Child Of The Sun

A Historical Novel Based on the Journey
of Cabeza de Vaca across North America

by

FRANK CHEAVENS, PH.D.

Illustrations by Buck (J.M.) Cheavens and Ted Cheavens

SUN BOOKS
Sun Publishing Company

First Sun Books Printing..1986 Feb

Dedicated to:
John and Lynda, and their children
Carolyn, John Dwain, Ted, and Emily

Copyright © 1985 by Frank Cheavens

Order from Sun Books
Sun Publishing Company, P.O. Box 5588
Santa Fe, NM 87502-5588

Hardback   ISBN: 0-89540-157-6
Paperback   ISBN:0-89540-161-4
Printed in the United States of America

The Prologue
of Cazador the Narrator

Every book should have valid reasons for being written. Here at the beginning are mine for writing this.

As I look at myself and the changes that have taken place in me and my way of life, I am convinced that this is one of my chief reasons for writing. I was from the Pueblo Indians on the Tiguex River. For reasons I shall tell later I was considered to be subnormal physically by my people. I became an itinerant trader. And now, when I see what my life is, I realize the great transformation that has taken place. It is the difference between stumbling in darkness and walking in the fullness of daylight.

How did this new life, my new attitudes and new ways of thinking, come about? Largely, the creative path that my feet took was due to one man, Álvar Núñez Cabeza de Vaca, whom we aptly called the Child of the Sun. However, often as I think of him, an even better name occurs—Child of the Great Spirit.

There had been great alterations in the attitudes, thinking, and behavior of Cabeza de Vaca, himself. I did not know him before these took place. However, he told me about them during the winter we spent at the village of the Avavares Indians. What I saw was the new Cabeza de Vaca and the very unusual results of his new attitude toward the Indians.

I think that this transformation of man's attitudes and thinking are the most difficult and the most important of all. But many times physical changes seem to us more spectacular. I was certainly not exempt from this overemphasis on the physical, although now I know it is only symbolic of more subtle, invisible events within the person.

This book is casually the story of several significant years of my life. But the real import of the story is what happened to Álvar Núñez Cabeza de Vaca and what happened through him during his strange and wonderful journey from the Gulf of Mexico to the west coast of Mexico to Culiacán. The physical events of that journey would have been unbelievable to me if I had not seen them happen.

Nearly everything I have heard about him and read about him emphasized his feats of exploration. He was the first European to cross the North American continent. This was an unusual achievement, and he deserves a great deal of credit for his hardihood, perseverance, and success in accomplishing it. But greater still, and one of my chief reasons for writing this, was his altruism toward the Indians and his service of helping and healing among them. Not the least of the results of this altruism was that he succeeded in stopping the vicious practice of slave-hunting and -trading in Mexico.

Certain sequels to his journey across North America should be recounted. I have been in a position to know about these and shall tell them as fully as I can. Perhaps the chief reason I feel compelled to write this is because of my great indebtedness.

My gratitude toward Núñez, as his friends called him, goes even further. Through him and his teaching I was changed from an unlettered Pueblo commercial trader to an educated teacher. But more important still, what I know of the spiritual life came from him.

Preface

While this is a work of fiction, based upon a narrator who is fictional, it is built around a series of historical events that are not fictional. The journey of Álvar Núñez Cabeza de Vaca and his three companions, the first Europeans to cross continental North America, is factual and well-authenticated history. I have been as accurate as I know how to be in the reproduction of the factual elements.

Thus, the factual framework of what follows is based upon the journal of Cabeza de Vaca himself and the "joint report" that was written by Cabeza de Vaca, Dorantes, and Castillo in Mexico City. This joint report has been lost, but the historian of early Mexico, Gonzalo Fernández de Oviédo y Valdez, had access to it and summarized it in his history.

The journals in Spanish are available. Fortunately, I can read the Spanish with facility. The two major translations of the original journals into English were made first by Thomas Buckingham Smith in 1851 and later in 1905 by Fanny Bandelier.

The best summary and analysis of the journey was written by Cleve Hallenbeck. In his book he depended upon Dr. Carl Sauer, geographer, and professor emeritus at the University of California at Berkeley, for the section treating Cabeza de Vaca's journey in western Mexico, from what is now northern Sonora to Culiacán. These men are familiar with Cabeza de Vaca's route, from both scholarly research and extensive personal travel and experience with the parts of the route about which they write.

There have been two generally adequate factual accounts of Cabeza de Vaca's journeys. One of these was Morris Bishop's *Odyssey of Cabeza de Vaca* in 1933. The other was John Upton Terrell's *Journey into Darkness* in 1962. Both of these contain certain fundamental errors in de Vaca's route, according to the most accurate research and scholarship coupled with wide personal observation and experience.

My fascination with all aspects of this remarkable man, Álvar Núñez Cabeza de Vaca, and his service to the Indians stimulated me to write this work of fiction.

Chapter I
Before I Met
The Child of the Sun

For several years I was a trader between Indian villages, and this was the way I happened to fall into that life. I am what the Spaniards call a Pueblo by birth. I was born in the farthest south of any of the Pueblo villages on the Great River of the north, which the Spaniards later called the *Rio Grande del Norte.*

You see, I am a dwarf. When I should have grown tall, my head grew large, and my shoulders and arms big and strong, and my torso also strong. But my legs remained very short. They, too, were strong and vital, but they just did not grow long enough.

My name is Sannetos, but I shall not mention it again. I am affected by the superstition of my people that to call a person's name very much weakens him. Most of us go by nicknames. At an unusually early age I learned to snare rabbits. I caught so many that it became hard to give them away. Also I became skilled with the bow and arrow. This is how I earned my nickname Hunter. Later Álvar Núñez Cabeza de Vaca and his companions called me Cazador.

In those early days none of us knew there were any such people as the Spaniards. We knew there were many different tribes

of Indians, and that a great number of them looked different and
spoke different languages, but we never dreamed there were any
people as different as the Spaniards, and of course I had no idea
there was such a man in the world as Álvar Núñez Cabeza de
Vaca.

Sometime after my 15th year, it became plain that my legs
were abnormally short. While I knew my mother and brothers
and sisters loved me, I began to sense also that they were ashamed
of me. This, then, made me ashamed of myself.

The Pueblos were in the north. My people were handsome to
look at, wise in the ways of the mountains, of the forest and of the
plains. They knew much about both men and animals. They
never waged war unless it was to defend themselves. They were
skilled in the use of weapons, especially the bow and arrow, but
also the spear. For protection against enemies they made shields
of tough hides of buffalos.

My people also knew the art of growing their own food, especially the large-kerneled corn, but also squash, beans, and onions.
They had domesticated turkeys. They were superior hunters,
killing deer and many other animals for food and clothing. Their
clothing was also made of cotton which they cultivated. Need-
less to say, I was proud of my people.

One day, Donash, the shaman of our village whom I liked very
much, called me to him. "Hunter, I would have a long talk with
you in the Kiva."

"When, Medicine Man?"

"Could you come this afternoon?" I assured him I could.

That afternoon, I found him waiting for me in the circular
Kiva. At first he did not see me and his eyes seemed fixed far
away. Many times he seemed to be seeing things the rest of us
were blind to. I waited respectfully, because I knew this man's
spirit took strange journeys. At last he became aware of me.
From his eyes, it was as if he were returning from another world.

"I'm glad you came, Hunter. You have been much in my
thoughts. I wanted to speak to you because certain knowledge
has been given to me which is important to you."

I wondered at this strange statement. "I know your problem,"
he said. "You are sad and ashamed because you are different

from others. But you need not be, because you can make a better life for yourself than any of our people."

"I do not understand how this can be. I cannot compete with other men. No woman will have me as her husband."

Donash waited long before speaking.

"Hunter, you learn quickly and as well as anyone I have ever known. You are skilled in tracking and hunting. You can train a dog better than anyone in the village. You have learned the language of signs better than any of our young men."

"This I know, Donash, yet what I said is true. Am I to live alone all my life, with no woman in the lodge* to give me companionship, to make a home for me, and give me children?"

Again he waited long to answer. I could feel the great kindness in his voice as he told me, "Hunter, every man who enters the world is different from every other man, and his destiny is different. What you say is true, but you can still have a good life."

"But how, Donash? I do not see how."

"Yes, there is a way. You may become a trader. Our women sometimes trade even with enemy tribes, because a woman is never a threat. So they can travel in safety. You, because of your smallness, can do the same thing. You can travel far and see more and learn more than any of our people. You can be accepted by tribes everywhere and be liked by everyone. You also have an attitude of helpfulness. Others will always help you because of this. Think on this, Hunter, and if you decide this is right for you, all of us will help you so that you will be well equipped when you start."

Then I told him, "I will think on what you say and will let you know."

For many days following the shaman's message to me I thought about it from every angle. I wanted to get away from the shame my family felt about me. I knew my mother loved me, but was still ashamed of me. My father was the only one in our family who had completely accepted me. I began to feel I must leave my family and my village. So I went to the shaman. "Your way is

---

*Traditionally the Pueblo woman was owner of the lodge.

best," I told him. "I shall become a wanderer on the face of the earth."

"You shall be of greater service to all people than any of our tribe. You are a special person. Did you know there are tribes that reverence and even fear anyone who is a dwarf?"

I laughed harshly. "I hope in my wanderings I can find those people."

"You will find them, never fear," he assured me.

In my family, my father was the only one to whom I divulged my plan, as well as what the shaman had told me. "It hurts me to lose you, Son. Of all my children, you are my favorite. But you must find your own way in life, as each of us must, and no two lives can be the same."

My father began to help me make preparations for leaving. First he found for me a good dog, better than I ever dreamed a dog could be. His name was Bolo and he was only eight months old when my father gave him to me. He was large, and looked very much like a gray wolf, although he was gentle and friendly. He learned to hunt quickly and to obey me and help me in many ways. In a short time we became constant companions.

Next my father and Donash constructed a sledge* for me. They made it of light, strong poles. On the ends that dragged on the ground, they glued the curved horns of a buffalo which they told me would last a very long time and could be easily replaced. They made a harness for Bolo and I began to teach him to pull my sledge, which he could do easily.

My mother wept openly as she told me good-bye. But it was my father who I knew was really supporting me, as well as the medicine man who seemed to have some knowledge of my future.

I made my way southward through a long stretch of desolate country. Its unfriendliness could have been deadly if the traveler did not know his way. But I knew the right trails to take and also the one place in the long stretch where water was available. Here I stopped to refill my good waterbag. I also knew which of the cactus were best if I had to cut them open for water. It was

---

*This was what the French later called a *travois.*

My father found me a good dog, eight months old.

the spring of the year and was still cool in the high Pueblo country. This made my journey over this barren stretch to the east of the Great River not as uncomfortable as it would have been in hot weather.

In my unaccustomed loneliness on this desolate part of my journey, I had much time to think. Chiefly my mind came back many times to Donash, the shaman of our village. What made him such an unusual person?

I thought that perhaps the answer lay in his knowledge of the Great Spirit, because it was commonly known among us that this was the whole of his life. This was unusual for a Pueblo shaman, because our religion has little to say about this. But Donash had spent several years wandering among many tribes and, from some of their shamans, he had acquired this belief that became of great importance to him.

Many times I had heard him speak of the Great Spirit. And, while I believed what he said was true, mine was largely an intellectual belief. I had a clear recollection of his teaching—that the Great Spirit was in everything and had created everything. He said that the Great Spirit was in us, too. Mentally, I felt this was true. But this Great Spirit had seemed far away, very remote from my life.

I know that this was not true of Donash. It was said by our people that Donash was in constant touch with the Great Spirit and that he was possessed by Him.

Yet for me this was not so. My life was filled with the real problems of daily living. It was also filled with a feeling of deprivation, because of my size and because I was very different from most people.

Even so, it was good to know there were such people as Donash. It appeared that he never worried about himself; his thoughts were always for showing other people how to help themselves. All the problems of my life and my future had been of great importance to him.

So here I was on my journey because of Donash. It gave me a feeling that this life was right for me at this particular time. I long ago had learned to trot in my travel whenever a path became smooth. This way I could cover great distances. In almost three days I crossed this barren country which the Spaniards later called *el Jornado del Muerto* (the Journey of the Dead One) and came to a Suma village not far from the southern mouth of a steep canyon of the Great River. I found that the Suma people received me well.

My father had given me many fine turquoise stones before I left and the Sumas were eager to own them. So my trading went well and I loaded my sledge with merchandise that would be needed by the people farther south.

I followed the Great River southward from village to village, coming next to the Jumano tribe, who spoke the same language as the Sumas but were unfriendly toward them.

I had heard of the salt lakes to the east and guided my journey toward a great round mountain, following a trail that led past waterholes. I sighted other high mountains to the east and followed a trail pointing south of these to the salt lakes. Each night I stopped at a watering-place where there were always lodges of Indians who were friendly to me. At the salt lakes, I loaded as much salt on my sledge as Bolo could pull conveniently. I also loaded salt on a pack strapped to my shoulders.

I crossed a river which the Indians called the River of the Buffalos, * since many hunters traveled up the stream toward the buffalo country in hunting season. I cut across to still another river flowing east and followed the trail until it merged with a still longer stream running south. I had left the mountains far behind and was now in hilly country. My salt had been much in demand and was now all gone, replaced by lighter merchandise—such as the wooden combs I had learned how to make. These were greatly desired by both men and women, equally intent upon having their hair well groomed.

Summer and hot weather had begun and I still kept traveling on trails leading eastward. By midsummer I arrived at the junction of two rivers—a small clear stream and a larger stream which, because of summer rains, was muddy. The people that lived here were the Chorrucas and it was at this village that I first

---

*This was the Pecos River, also called by the Indians the River of Bitter Water.

heard of a trader who was also a healer, called by the name of Núñez. Later I learned that his full name was Álvar Núñez Cabeza de Vaca and that he had spent two winters in the Chorrucas' village. I liked the village and, tired of traveling, decided to spend time here. Their language, kin to that of my people, came easily and soon I was able to speak it fairly well. I was good in the use of the sign language, a common language between all tribes, and had used this language of signs with every tribe on my journey. But now I found pleasure in learning the Chorruca tongue and speaking it.

I traded in villages in the surrounding country where the same language as that of the Chorrucas was spoken. I was deeply interested in all the different tribes and observant of all the country through which I traveled. In my times of solitude, the memory of the shame of my mother and brothers and sisters was an unhappy one. Also my feeling that any woman would be ashamed to take me as a husband made me feel unwanted and desolate.

I heard Núñez spoken of in all these villages. The people said he had been sent from heaven, that he was a child of the sun and could perform miracles of healing. The more I heard of him the more I wanted to meet him.

Chapter II

Sunrise: My First Meeting
With the Child of the Sun

I heard that Núñez was trading in the Caddo country, so I decided to journey that way. The farther east I went, the more the houses seemed to be permanent. They were mostly built of strong poles, and the roofs were thatched, many times shaped like pointed cones, the better to shed water. There was more rain in this forested eastern country. Most of the villages had long meeting houses that served the same purpose as our Kivas. The people had fine gardens of corn, squash and beans. This was a land of tall pine trees and big hardwoods. It was spring and the abundance of dogwood filled the woods with clouds of filmy white. Many redbuds also added their cheerful color.

Bolo was a good companion. He was the best small game dog I had ever known. In the villages, he would never pick fights with the other dogs, but he could defend himself against the worst of them.

From village to village I went, always trading and befriending all the people I could. In every village Núñez was spoken of with awe and reverence.

One day, as I was walking through pine-covered hills, I came to a rocky bluff from which the eye could travel long distances from ridge to misty ridge, becoming dim on the horizon. On a rocky promontory I saw a man standing, gazing across the valleys. As I drew closer, I knew it was Núñez—from the lightness of his skin and the blackness of his hair, not only on his scalp but covering his jaws and chin. Like most Indian men he was naked, except for a breechclout. He seemed lost in the view before him but turned when he saw me, and I could sense his good feeling toward me.

As I went to him, without planning to I found myself kneeling before him and felt his hand on my head, as if in friendship. Then, as I stood and looked into his large, dark eyes and the fine features of his face, I sensed a sort of radiance that I had never felt before.

I knew he spoke the Chorruca tongue, so I said to him, "My people to the far north call me Hunter, and I greet you. I am a trader."

"I too am a trader and I welcome your company. Let us travel together. It is good to become friends. Your name in my language would be *Cazador.* I shall call you that." I liked the sound of the name, and was called that until I later visited the Ópatas.

I became aware that he was a beautiful being, tall, straight and well formed. But he was thin, very thin. I knew he did not eat enough strengthening food and I made up my mind to remedy that.

"Bolo," I said, "go get us some meat." Bolo knew exactly what I wanted and raced off through the brush. Núñez and I made our way down a steep path toward the valley below. We walked until we came to a clear creek with sandy beaches and there made our fire and camped. Bolo brought us one fat rabbit and raced off to get another. With a sharp obsidian knife I skinned the animal and we began to broil its meat. Núñez ate hungrily. When Bolo brought me a young raccoon, I skinned and cleaned it, too, and we ate part of it, saving some back for morning.

When we were satisfied, we sat long by the fire and talked. This was the beginning of the most wonderful thing that had ever happened to me, a friendship that opened a new life to me. I felt liked and comfortable with Núñez from the start, no matter how great a man he was.

The next day as we journeyed, I was full of questions. "Master, all the villagers say you come from above, that you are a child of the sun. Where is your home? Where do you come from?"

"My homeland is far, far away," he answered sadly, "and I am homesick for it and for my people. It is a land called *La España* and lies across a water so big, so wide, that even in a big boat the sailor feels lost upon it. For days and days you can sail and sail and see no land."

I tried to imagine this and could not. I had seen big rivers and lakes, but they were always closed in by land. It was not that I doubted Núñez. It was that I could not picture what he was describing.

He went on talking. "We have little people like you in my land. We call them *enanos* if they are men and *enanas* if they are women."

"You mean there are small women, too? This I have never heard of."

"Yes," he said, "there are just as many small women as small men."

"No women in our villages are small, and none would think of having me for a husband. That is why I became a trader."

"I have not seen my wife for many years. So we are both alone. Except that *el Bendito Dios* is with us all the time."

"*Dios?* I do not understand."

"You call Him the Great Spirit. He is called by different names, but He is the same being." His large, dark eyes took on a luminous quality as he talked about the Great Spirit.

"But you used another word, too."

"I said '*el Bendito Dios.*' That means that the Great Spirit is blessed and loving."

"My people believe that the Great Spirit is everything. The Chorrucas say you come from the sky and are a child of the sun."

"That is because they have never seen a man like me before, and because their sick are healed when I pray for them."

"They say you work miracles and perform magic."

"It is true that many wonderful things have happened, things that surprised me. But if the sick have been healed, it has not been I that have healed them, but the Great Spirit that did the healing."

"But they say you and the Great Spirit talk to each other, and that you are His son."

"I am His son only as all men who believe in Him are His sons. And it is true I talk with Him. We call it prayer. I ask Him to bless the people. It is because He hears my prayers that the sick are healed."

"But they say He talks to you."

"He talks to me as He talks to all men, with His love and His goodness in my mind and my heart."

"The Chorrucas say you make magic signs over the sick, and that you are a magician."

"The sign that I make over the sick is the sign of the cross. Later I shall tell you all about it. The sign of the cross is a sign that means God's love. And in one way God's great love is always magic as it lives in us."

Núñez knew the sign language well and at times used it to help explain his meaning.

We breakfasted on the remains of our cooked rabbits and the raccoon we had saved for that purpose. Bolo caught two more rabbits for us before we ate again at noon. Before he ate at each meal, Núñez made the sign of the cross, closed his eyes and said words I did not understand.

When he saw me looking at him questioningly, he said, "The words are the words of a prayer that a great teacher, Jesu-Cristo, taught his disciples many years ago to say. In my language we call it *El Padre Nuestro*, which means the Great Spirit is our Father. I will teach you the words of this prayer. Would you like to learn my language?"

I told him I would, so he began to teach me many of his words. I learned the word for rabbit was *"el coñeja."* He taught me a verse from a book called *La Biblia*. The verse used the words *"Dios es amor"* (God is love).

That night as we camped he asked me, "We have something we call *'escribir'* (to write). You will wish to learn this. I will show you."

He took a big strip of light-colored bark and made marks upon it with a piece of ochre.

"These marks say *'Dios es amor.'"*

"I do not understand."

"You know the language of signs. Each sign means something. These marks, *'Dios es amor,'* mean that the Great Spirit is your friend, that He loves you. See if you can make these marks."

I took a piece of ochre and slowly made the same marks he had made.

"You can do it!" he exclaimed laughingly. "You can learn to write. If you make those marks, I know it means the Great Spirit is my friend."

He made more marks. "These marks mean *'el coñejo,'* which is a rabbit in my language. You can make marks just like mine."

So I slowly copied his marks. "You did it again!" he shouted. "You can learn to write."

He then made more marks on the bark and I copied them. "It is magic!" I said.

"No," he replied. "I'm sure you know how to track animals and men."

"Yes, I learned this from early boyhood. My father was a good teacher."

"These marks I make are like making tracks. You follow them to ideas. It is a way of talking without making a sound."

We walked to a high riverbank where we found deposits of ochre. Núñez started filling his big bag that was strapped to his back. I began loading my sledge.

"You need a sledge like mine," I told him.

"It would be great trouble to drag."

"Not if you had a big strong dog like Bolo."

"If I had a dog, I would have to feed him. I wish to keep my life simple. When I am alone, food is always a problem."

"Bolo is a hunting dog. He brings me meat every day."

"I would have a hard time finding a dog as good as yours."

Núñez and I spent an entire month together. We visited a few villages and traded. Since food was now no problem for him, Núñez was indifferent about the villages and trading, and preferred to spend our time together teaching me. He taught me important Spanish sentences about food and work and religion.

Among many words I learned to write was my name in Spanish, *Cazador.*

In that time we became fast friends. But he had been asked by neighboring villages to go to the southwest, where there were sick who needed healing. I wanted to go north and later return to the Chorruca village before cold weather.

"Will you winter in the Chorruca village?" I asked him.

"It depends upon the needs of the villages I go to. Unless I feel there are villages that need me, I shall try to meet you in the Chorruca village. But I must go where I am needed most. Also, one of my countrymen is still the slave of the Indians on the island. I must see him and persuade him to leave his masters and go with me to see our countrymen. His name is Ovièdo."

"Why has he not escaped long ago?"

"He is a fearful man. He thinks only of the dangers of such a journey. Fear is his worst master, not the coastal Indians."

Chapter III

My Search for a Gift
for the Child of the Sun

One of the reasons why I wanted to go north was to visit the
country where there were many buffalo robes. I had noticed that
Núñez had only deerskins sewn together to sleep on at night. I
wanted to get him two of the best buffalo robes so that when cold
weather came he could sleep comfortably. It was not the season
to hunt the buffalo, but I could always trade for the robes which
would be plentiful farther north.

So I journeyed northwest, away from the pine forests and across
a river with red water running over sand and with many sand-
bars. Since I wanted to travel fast, I avoided most of the villages.

More than ever before I noticed the beauty of everything that
lay about me—the tall, green cottonwood trees with their flut-
tering leaves making a soft clattering sound, the startling white
of the herons along the river. And as I came into open country
the sunset seemed like color slashed across the sky by a giant
hand. Had my new consciousness of the presence of the Great
Spirit made my eyes keener to perceive the beauty of all things?
I noticed the grace of the deer as they ran and their rhythm as
they jumped over bushes obstructing their way. I saw the alert-

ness and aliveness of the coyotes as they ran from me.

I followed a tributary of the red-colored river, and found a clear lake made by the overflow of the stream. I felt that there would be fish in the small lake. So, being fish-hungry, I took out my small bone hook and line of sinews and cut a willow pole. I found snails on the limbs of bushes, which I used as bait. As I expected, there were catfish in the lake. I caught two and cleaned them and put them in thick shade where the fresh air could strike them. This way they would stay cool and firm for a long time.

I heard a noise behind me and looked back to see the beautiful face of a young woman, peering at me through the green leaves of a willow bush. She had soft, dark eyes, very large. I noticed her eyes first. Then I saw she had full lips that looked as if she smiled a great deal. She had high cheekbones, and a small nose. Mostly it was a friendly, generous face, which is even better than being pretty.

"Boy," she said in sign language, "are you catching any fish?" She came from behind the willow and stood beside me, and I could see she was well formed, with strong fine legs showing underneath her short deerskin skirt. And a pleasant fullness was apparent under her clean, cotton blouse.

"I am not a boy," I told her. "I am a man." I, too, used sign language.

She looked at me more closely and remarked, "I have never seen a man as small as you." There was no unkindness in her words as she said this. She was just honest in expressing her feeling.

"It is because I am so small that I became a trader." I pointed at my sledge and its merchandise. "I knew none of the women of my village would have me as a husband."

"You have a good face and head, and strong shoulders and body. It is only that your legs are very short." She said no more about me and I knew that she was a kind, sweet person.

"My name is Cazador," I told her.

"And mine is Nalla. You have caught two nice fish. Where do you come from?" As she asked this I could sense her liking for me. So I explained that I was from the Pueblos along the Great River, but had gone far south in my trading, and then turned north because I wanted two good buffalo robes for a great man who was a teacher and healer. I was surprised when she said that her village had heard of this strange white man who was a great healer. As we talked, more and more I could see how attractive Nalla was.

"And where do you come from?" I asked her.

"I have been to see my sister in her village to the east. Now I am returning home."

"Are you not afraid to travel alone?"

She shook her head. "This is safe country. There is no one among any of our villages that would harm me."

"How far is your village?"

"Half a day's journey."

"But it is late. You are not going to walk at night, are you?"

Again she shook her head. "Nearby is a place where I can sleep comfortably between our villages. Soon I will show you." She smiled and pointed at the fish. "Let me cook them for us?"

I nodded my consent. She skillfully started a fire with dry grass, bark and twigs that caught flame from two flints which, when struck together, made large sparks. Nalla did this as quickly as anyone I had ever seen.

She broiled one fish, and offered it to me. I took a pinch of its juicy meat and gave the whole fish to Nalla. She ate it with great pleasure, licking her fingers after she had picked every crumb of flesh from the bones. She then started broiling the other fish.

Meanwhile Bolo had brought me a rabbit, which I skinned and cleaned with my good obsidian knife. When Nalla had finished broiling the second catfish, again she gave it to me. I took a pinch of it, ate it and returned the whole fish to her. She laughed out loud. "I like fish!" She proceeded to eat the second fish and pick its bones. So I cooked my rabbit and ate it, although I like fish better. How I enjoyed watching Nalla devour my two big catfish. And what a good appetite she had, for when I offered her part of my rabbit she ate that too.

Nalla made friends with Bolo quickly, scratching behind his ears. I was seated on a large rock and Nalla came and sat beside me. "I like you," she said. "You are nice." Her soft hands reached my cheek and caressed it lightly. My arm encircled her pliable

body. I drew her close to me. She leaned her head against mine.
"You are a beautiful girl."

She turned her face toward mine and did something very few
Indian women do. She pressed her full lips against mine. It was
so sweet, I wanted her to do it again and again. We sat for a long
time caressing each other, and enjoying it. It was growing dark.

"Come," she said, "and I will show you the place where we
shall sleep." She caught my hand and led me through an opening in the bushes to a small lodge built as protection against
rain, wind or cold. Held high by leather thongs were two buffalo
robes. Nalla untied these and shook them out and spread one of
them over the mats on the floor. Bolo nestled down outside the
opening of the shelter.

Nalla and I lay together on the comfortable robe. The night
was growing cool, so we pulled the other robe over us. The feeling of this fine girl beside me was delicious. Without embarrass-
ment, she made love to me, and my experience with her was
ecstatic. We awakened during the night to make love again, and
did not arise until the sun shown through the doorway on our
faces.

"You are a wonderful lover," she said. "And I can tell you are
a good man and would make a good husband. I wish we could be
together always, because I like you better than any man I have
known. But I can't. Many young men in my village want me.
They would make trouble. And the other women would make
fun of me, saying that I, a grown woman, had married a little
boy. I wouldn't want that to happen to me, nor to you."

I knew that what Nalla said was true, as hard as it was for me
to acknowledge it.

So Nalla left me, and I saw tears in her eyes as she told me
good-bye. "These are my own buffalo robes and I want you to
have them. Take them with you and think of what our love
might have become if we had known each other longer." She left
quickly.

I took these two good robes. It was what I had come for. I turned
my face in the direction of the Chorrucas again.

My lovemaking with Nalla had been very good, even rap-
turous. Yet it left me dissatisfied and bitter. No matter how

pleasurable it had been, this was not what I really wanted. The physical part of our lovemaking had been very good, but it was not enough. The union of the bodies of men and women should be the symbol of their friendship for each other and of a close companionship and loyalty. So I was sad as I went toward the southeast.

I stopped at a village the other side of the red river and found the people friendly. It was here I met an unusual Indian. He was fearless, an adventurer. He had traveled far. He was expert with bow and arrow and spear. He was known as a great hunter. His name was Dallan.

A number of men had gathered in the meeting lodge to hear Dallan tell of his travels. "I journeyed to the edge of a big water far to the west. You could look west over this water and see no land at all. There was only water, water, as far as the eye could see."

I thought of Núñez telling me of sailing in a boat on a similar water.

"The water was salty and bitter and no man could drink it. It was full of fish, big fish, which I caught in abundance and gave to the people who were befriending me. Where I sensed danger, I avoided the people. Where I found friendliness, I hunted and fished for them and helped them with their work. In the jungles along the rivers, there were big spotted cats. I killed one of these and here is the skin." He unrolled the pelt of a large animal that I was later to hear the Spaniards call *el tigre.* *

Before he went to the lodge where he was to spend the night, he said to me, "Cazador, I would like to talk with you."

I went with him out under the stars.

"What I wanted to tell you about was a woman I met in one of the villages. These people were called the Cáhitas. All the people of this country spoke a language called the Pima. At first when I saw this woman, I thought she was just a beautiful little girl. But when I looked more closely at her, I saw she was a well-developed woman, but small like you."

*The jaguar

"An Indian woman who is a dwarf?" This news excited me.

"Yes, and no man in the village would take her for a wife. She was so small they thought she could not do the hard work of a good wife."

"And yet I, a dwarf, am stronger than many large, tall men."

"She seemed to be not only a beautiful woman, but a loving, good one. She had a younger sister who was even then about as tall as she. The name of this dwarf woman is Muna. I think you would like to know her. She would make you a good wife."

"Tell me where this village is." I was eager to find out all I could about this small woman.

Dallan drew me a map on the ground in the light of a fire in front of his lodge. The land where she lived was far to the west, much farther than even my own village in the Pueblos. I studied his map and directions until I could never forget them. Right there I made up my mind I would travel to the distant western country to find this woman whom Dallan had seen.

I remembered Núñez telling me that in his country there were dwarf women as well as men. Perhaps I would some day find a wife. It was with this thought that the next day I traveled rapidly south toward the village of the Chorrucas.

Chapter IV
The Child of the Sun Escapes

When I came to the Chorruca village I found that Núñez had been there but had taken a trip toward the coast to the Island of Bad Luck, the place where the Spaniards had first been cast ashore. He had told me about Ovièdo, his countryman, who still remained on this island as a slave to the Indians. I had a feeling that Núñez was again trying to get Ovièdo to go with him as he started the search for his countrymen.

As much as I disliked going among the barbarous coastal Indians, I had acquired a heavy load of flint to trade. The coastal Indians were always in short supply of flint, so I decided the most practical thing for me to do was to get to the coast in hopes of meeting Núñez and to trade my flint for shells, sea-beans, and other merchandise that was always in demand inland. Núñez had fully informed me about the coastal Indians.

So I made my way to the coast. I was determined to get a view of the big water Núñez had told met about, but which I could not picture. Once again Bolo and I followed trails leading through tall pines and great hardwoods. I now traveled fast, and in a few weeks found the forest thinning and the coastal plains studded with clumps of oaks. Fortunately, there were well marked trails and I was able at low tide to cross to the island on its southern end.

I spent many days trading and loaded my sledge with coral and pretty shells. Also I traded for as many of the big sea-beans as were available. It was true that these coastal tribes were more barbarous than other Indians. But I managed to get along well with them. In telling me about his experiences with them, Núñez had said that they were very kind to their children and this I found to be true.

I stood for the first time on a sandy beach looking eastward toward water as far as the eye could travel, which was the distant horizon. The water was green and clear where the waves swept up on the beaches and in the distance, as far as I could see, it was still green. The Indians told me that when the weather was bad, it turned brown and muddy.

I watched the water birds, gulls and terns, and great pelicans, both white and brown. There were many ducks and geese. This was now the season for them to come from their northern home to southern waters where they spent the winter. I hunted much, set my snares, and went over all the lessons Núñez had given me until I knew them well from memory. I also practiced the writing that I had learned until I could do it well. I practiced even as I journeyed back to the Chorrucas. I was now able to write all the Spanish letters clearly and accurately and quickly. And many times when I was alone, I spoke what Spanish I knew out loud and with the clear memory of how Núñez's speech had sounded.

In the spring I was surprised when the Chorrucas told me a messenger wanted to see me. He was a man who had come from the south. He handed me a large piece of bark with words written on it in Spanish. And I could read them!

"Te encontraré en la fiesta de las tunas." (I shall see you during the feast of the tunas.) I, of course, knew about the great feast of the tunas. When the season came in the summer, this great feast was held in the large areas of the prickly-pears to the southwest. It was also a time of truce, when tribes that had been enemies forgot about their hostilities and met in peace among the prickly-pears to eat gluttonously of their fruit, the tuna, which

was both red and purplish when ripe.

I turned my face toward the southwest when the season came in the summer, with the great anticipation of being with Núñez again. And since I planned to travel north and west as I began my search for Muna, this suited me well.

I arrived at the great tuna grounds and found many people there. I began to enquire for Núñez. With everyone knowing about him, because of his work as a medicine man, I was able to find my way to him.

Núñez greeted me with a warm embrace. They called this *un abrazo.* And he gave me a second hug after the first. This I knew they called *el abrazo doble.* He was pleased when I gave him the two fine buffalo robes.

"I tried to get Ovièdo to leave his island slavery, but that man is afraid of everything. He leads a miserable life, but is afraid he will starve if he leaves the island. He traveled with me for a long way, and I thought at last I had persuaded him to seek for better things. And then he turned back to the barbarians of the coast and his servitude there. I cannot understand it! I can wait for Ovièdo no longer!

"Now I need to tell you my plans. Three of my countrymen are here, but they are all still slaves to the Indians from the coast. They will have to run away. And then the four of us are going to the north and the west, as far from the cruel coastal Indians as possible. If you miss me, you will know which way I have gone and can pick up my trail to the northwest."

"That suits me fine," I said to him. Then I told him about Muna and that I planned to hunt for her in the far west.

But the Spaniards were thwarted in their plan. A serious quarrel started between the families holding the three Spaniard slaves. So each family left the tuna field, taking their slave with them.

Núñez was disappointed and said to me, "We shall have to delay another year until the feast of the tuna next year. I know you received my message written on the bark."

"Yes, I can see how useful writing can be. I look forward to learning more. I shall go on with my trading until next year at this time."

The Indians were a heterogenius group as they harvested the tunas.

The delay of a year was hard for me take. Now I knew that my greatest loyalty was to Núñez. The happy idea of some day having a wife and a home of my own was not as strong as my need to be close to Núñez.

If I had known what was going to happen to him during that year of waiting, I think I could have done something to help him. But I lost track of him and did not see him again for a year. . .

When the next September we met again at the feast of the tuna, he told me he had been forced into slavery again and abused. But he had succeeded in escaping from his captors and making his way back to the tuna fields. This time the other two Spaniards, Dorantes and Castillo, and Dorantes' moorish slave, the dark, tall Estevánico, had succeeded in escaping from their masters and were expected to circle to the northwest of the tuna fields. Núñez told me where to pick up their trail and I found it easily.

I saw from their trail that they were traveling fast, no doubt in an effort to assure that they were not recaptured. I followed the trail with ease and was glad that no one else seemed to be following them. As I did not need to hurry, I camped alone that night with the comfort of my faithful Bolo close by.

The next day, their trail led to a village of lodges made with mats. As I entered it I found that the people here were called the Avavares, and that their language was almost the same as that of the Chorrucas.

Already the Spaniards had started their service of healing. Castillo, whom I was seeing for the first time, prayed and made the sign of the cross over those in pain, upon which they avowed that their pain left immediately. The whole village was buzzing with the talk of wonderful healing. The families of the sick showered the Spaniards with tunas and with venison.

Núñez took me to meet three companions. All of them seemed to be good men, and perhaps powerful, yet I felt from none of them the radiance I had always experienced with Núñez.

News of the healing quickly spread to the neighboring villages, and soon a stream of people came to the Spaniards for healing. Each person bringing a sick person also brought venison, and soon the Spaniards had more than they knew what to do with. Núñez shared this meat with all that were hungry.

I watched the Spaniards perform their healing. They would pray over every sick person, make the sign of the cross, and blow on each one. I watched as each recipient left, announcing that he was well.

Following this abundant healing, the Avavares feasted three days, dancing late into each night, expressing their great joy that such blessings had been bestowed upon them. I watched the dancing, but left early with Bolo, and spread my buffalo robes far enough from the village so I would not be bothered by the noise. With the abundant supply of venison that Núñez had given me, I was spared all hunting. I could cook the venison, eat, and go to sleep. After three days, the village quieted down. Núñez and the three who had escaped decided to spend the winter with the Avavares, who had offered to build lodges for them.

The village of the Avavares was in a beautiful place. It was just at the edge of hills covered with oak and cedar. Not far from the lodges was a clear, cold spring. This made a small river which ran into the River of Nuts,* a much larger river. The village was on a high bank, safe from the highest floodwaters. Up and down both streams were many large trees loaded with nuts.** With the coming of winter, these nuts in great abundance would be a plentiful source of food. There were fish in both rivers but the Avavares were poor fishermen. They hunted some, but were mediocre hunters. They depended on nuts, tunas, and other natural fruit.

I left the village of the Avavares for a few days to do some trading. In a week I returned to find Núñez emaciated and scratched. His feet were raw and bleeding.

"What happened to you?" I asked in consternation.

"When the Indians went looking for tunas, I was lost for five whole days. Every night I dug a long hole for my body, built a fire and scraped coals in the hole. Then I cleaned it out carefully and slept in the warm ground, covering my body with grass to keep

*The Colorado River of Texas
**Pecans

from freezing. Luckily, there was no cold north wind or I would have died. One night my grass cover caught fire and I came out of my hole so fast I wasn't burned. I found nothing to eat. I threw rocks at rabbits, but was too weak to throw with much force. But God had mercy on me and I found the village again to regain my strength."

This incident convinced me that Núñez was far from being skilled in survival. But it also looked as if something was taking care of him. When Núñez had fully recovered, the Spaniards started visiting many of the neighboring villages that invited them to come and heal their sick.

Everywhere the talk of the villages was about one thing—the miracles that were being performed by these bearded Spaniards.

Chapter V
What Happened to the Child of the Sun Before I Met Him

When the Spaniards decided to spend the winter of 1534 with the Avavares, I was impatient because of the delay in my journey westward. But I had previously settled in my mind that it was more important to stay close to Núñez than to speed up my own plans. I knew that the same loyalty existed now, but even stronger. So my decision to stay with the Avavares had really already been made.

During the cool weather of late fall and the colder weather of winter, my life grew to be one of great personal gain inwardly. The Spaniards continued with their work of healing as opportunity offered itself. Little trading was necessary for me now. I had made some wooden combs since they were always in demand.

Also I appointed myself to keep the Spaniards supplied with meat since the Avavares were indifferent hunters. I could always set my snares but Bolo, being the superior hunting dog that he was, saved me much work of this kind and brought me small game every day. Mostly he supplied me with rabbits that were always plentiful. But sometimes he brought a possum or a raccoon or an animal that was like a raccoon, a ring-tailed cat. My name Cazador was exactly right for me, since I spent many hours in successful hunting. There were fish in the River of Nuts which I caught from time to time—freshwater drum, catfish, and bass. The catfish were the best eating of all for my personal taste. Occasionally I would shoot fish with arrows and, before the water became too cold, swim into the river to recover both fish and arrow.

In the fall, the Spaniards gathered many of the nuts which fell from the tall pecan trees, but the supply was limited since all the Avavares gathered nuts.

There was a widow among the Avavares who did not choose to remarry. Living alone in her lodge, she welcomed me to visit her at any time. She was not beautiful like Nalla, but she was friendly and loving. Many times when I had more than enough meat I would take her some. She was like a mother to me, and my memory of her goodness lives with me to this day.

One day Núñez said to me, "We have in my country what we call *la escuela* (school). It is a place where children learn. And we also have what is called *el colegio* where older people learn. Since you learn our Spanish tongue so readily, I think we should have an hour or two of *la escuela* every day. I want to teach you much more Spanish and I would like for you to learn to speak it as well as we do, and to write also."

Every day after that I spent time learning Spanish. Núñez and I gathered smooth bark on which I wrote with a piece of ochre. Since I was with the Spaniards much of the time, I heard them talk and talked a great deal with them. So I learned from the others as well as from Núñez. When I was hunting I would whisper or speak the Spanish sentences softly as I walked, and in this way the process was accelerated.

One day I told Núñez, "I want to know all about how you and your friends came to this country and about the beginning of your work healing the Indians."

"Bueno!" he replied. "I shall tell you, and every time I use a word that you do not know, tell me and you shall learn to say it and write it. This is a good way to learn."

Núñez began. "We sailed in boats from across the big water, for many, many days. This was in the year 1527. Our chief was a man called Pánfilo Narvaez. He was a hard, selfish man. We heard many bad things about him. He had lived on a big island which we call Hispanola. * He had made the Indians slaves, and was responsible for killing many cruelly when he was the commander of soldiers."

"Why did you come on this long, hard journey and under such a bad man?"

"We all came for different reasons. Some wanted gold, the yellow, soft metal you know about. It is very valuable in our land. Others came for excitement and adventure. A few felt they might get great fame or renown. I suppose I came because I thought it was my destiny."

I had to stop Núñez frequently to let him explain words and spell them. I had many pieces of bark to write on. I was becoming better all the time with writing. The word "destiny" was one that the shaman had used, and my father, also.

"We had four *padres* (priests) who came to teach the Indians about God and His son, Jesus. Also they were to help us be better Catholics. This is our religion.

"Narvaez was a poor leader. We came across the sea in big ships. These were our homes. We landed on April 4, 1528 on the west shores of a place named Florida. Narvaez foolishly, and against my counsel, left the boats which were our safety and let them return to Cuba and journeyed overland toward a village called Apalachen because he thought there were riches there. The natives shot arrows at us from woods on our overland journey and killed a few of our men every day. Also, we were short of food and were not good hunters."

Núñez was giving me good pictures of their travel and hardships. He then came to something that was completely strange to me.

"Some of our soldiers rode horses, large animals that we sit on comfortably." He stopped and on a piece of bark roughly drew a picture of this strange animal, and then wrote the word *caballo*. "Apalachen had no riches. Almost all of the natives did not want

*Cuba

us in their country. Because of this, they fought us constantly."

"Did you cure their sick?"

"We knew nothing about this."

"Did not your priests heal the sick?"

"They are not *curanderos* (medicine man) like your priests. They only teach about our religion. From Apalachen we started back to the sea, thinking that our escape might be that way. We were shot at all the way, and more men were killed. Some died of sickness. We were always hungry, very hungry.

"When we came to the sea, we knew we had to have boats to escape by water. We killed the horses that had grown very thin and were starving anyway. Thin as they were, our men ate their meat and were strengthened. The thought of horse meat repelled me, so I ate none."

"Then what did you live on?"

"The Indians grew corn and at every friendly village we traded bells and beads for corn. Or sometimes we just took it! I had little to eat but corn for many days. We had to build boats. We used the skin of the horses and one carpenter of our force supervised the building of five boats, each to hold fifty men! We melted metal we had and made crude oarlocks. It was hard work and none of us was skilled, but finally we went to sea in five boats, staying within sight of land.* Our boats had freeboard that was only six inches from the water. You can easily see the danger.

"We had much trouble with warlike Indians and always great difficulty getting food. For over a month we rowed and sailed along the coast, sometimes very thirsty, always hungry and constantly in danger from warlike Indians."

After Núñez revealed an episode of his travel, I would repeat it in Spanish to myself while out hunting with Bolo. I would practice retelling his story as nearly as possible using the exact words of Núñez himself. In this way my knowledge of Spanish kept growing at a fast pace. Every day I spoke little except in Spanish.

---

*De Soto later found the spot on the Florida coast, identified by the skulls and skeletons of horses that had been killed.

Soon after, Núñez continued his story. "After many hardships and battles and the loss of many men, our boats were caught by the strong current of a big river * and carried far out to sea. At the same time a fresh north wind also blew us out of sight of land. With sails made out of our shirts and with the help of our oars we tried to go in the direction of land. The boats lost sight of each other.

"My crew sighted Narvaez and his men and finally drew close enough to talk with them. I suggested that my boat be roped to his, since my men were now too weak to row and keep up with him. Narvaez refused, saying that it was now every boat for itself. He cared only for himself. Much later he and two of his companions were carried out to sea after they had landed. They were never seen again.

"One November night in 1528, when my men were weakened and benumbed from lack of food, we heard the sound of waves on the shore and were cast up on a sandy beach. All the men were jarred out of their stupor.

"The Indians proved to be friendly and brought us food for several days. When we had enough food saved to go to sea again, we tried to launch our boat and continue our journey. Since we had to get in the water to do this, we put all our clothes, and all else we had, in the boat. But the weather was cold and the water was beginning to be very cold and our hands were numb. So we could not use our oars well, and a big wave turned our boat over and threw us into the water. Three of our men were drowned. We lost our boat. It sank to the bottom. We swam back to the beach and, nearly frozen, rebuilt the coals of our fire and tried to warm ourselves.

"There the Indians found us, naked and shivering. But again they helped us and took us to their village. At the time, naked and defenseless, I felt utterly hopeless.

"Different families each took one Spaniard. They later made slaves of us to work for them. And the way we became medicine men was the strangest thing of all. The people asked us to cure

*This was probably the Mississippi.

their sick! We laughed at them."

"Laughed at them, Master? I do not understand you. You who are great healers laughed at them?"

"We laughed because we knew nothing of healing. As I told you, not even our priests are healers. Only certain men are trained in medicine.

"One shaman took me aside and reproved me, 'You must not laugh. Even some of our simple people can heal. They sometimes place a warmed rock on the aching stomach of a friend and cure the stomachache. You who are superior beings and wise can surely do the work of healing!'

"Even this did not show us the way. Then the Indians told us, 'If you will not be our medicine men, we will not feed you.' Castillo, Dorantes, and I talked this over. 'We are forced to be healers,' I said, 'or we will starve.'

"They told me, 'If you are willing to try healing, do so.'

"So I told the people of the island, 'Bring me your sick!' They did. I made the sign of the cross over them. Then I repeated the Lord's Prayer. I also said 'Ave Marias.' I also prayed as best I could to God to heal the sick. And like the Indian healers, I blew my breath on them. And the sick were healed! I was greatly surprised and so were my Spanish friends. From then on, we became healers from time to time. God has been good to us. From that first experience, we saw His power. And now we are seeing it more than ever, wherever we go."

This was a strange story Núñez had told me. These men now did almost nothing *but* heal. Yet only a few years before they knew nothing of it at all!

"Even though we cured their sick, the Indians still kept us as slaves. So I ran away to the Chorrucas, far inland, and became a trader and was a free man until others made me a slave again for the year just before our escape to this village. Even with the Chorrucas the news of my curing the sick on the coast had traveled ahead of me. They brought me all their sick in the Chorruca village.

"Again when I started as a trader, the news of this wonder that I myself could not explain went ahead of me. Some strange power was guiding me into a service for people that I had never dreamed of. This past year, when I became a slave again, the people still brought their sick to me for healing. Even when they were mistreating and abusing me, I still functioned as a healer. God's grace is upon me or it could never happen."

Before we parted, Núñez said to me, "You must get Dorantes to tell you what happened to them before we escaped from the feast of the tunas. He, Castillo, and Estevánico had some trying experiences. Dorantes, too, had an experience with the power of God."

Chapter VI
Did the Child of the Sun Bring the Dead Back to Life?

There was a village about a half day's journey away where the people called themselves Susolos. They spoke a language that was different from that of the Avavares. Messengers came from this village asking that the healers visit them to help their sick.

The messengers reported that one of the sick men was at the point of dying. They talked with Castillo first. He went to talk it over with Núñez and I heard their conversation.

"This is too hard for me. I do not feel that I should go. I am too great a sinner, and God might not hear my prayers. I am afraid I cannot give them the help they seek. I do not have enough faith for this task."

"Stay here, if you feel you should. I can go." Núñez was the most courageous of these men. He seemed never to fear to attempt the impossible.

As he left the village, I, Cazador, had to trail along with him. Dorantes went, too, and several of the Avavares along with the Susolo messengers. We went through hills covered with cedar and oak and came to the Susolo village, which was on a clear running creek that emptied into the same river on which the

Avavares village was located.

I saw many deer crashing through the brush as we went along the trail. My companions were too interested in getting to the sick to pay much attention to the game. I made up my mind that I would return to this area later for venison. As we walked I also noticed the birds—mockingbirds, cardinals, and several of the fast-running roadrunners.

When we reached the Susolo village, we found the people weeping. The man who had been so seriously sick had evidently already died. A woman told me in sign language, "It is too late. The man has died." They had already covered him with mats. The villagers were tearing his lodge down, which they always did when the owner died.

Núñez went to the man and uncovered his body. He felt for his pulse and I saw him sadly shake his head. He turned back the man's eyelids and again I saw him shake his head. Dorantes, too, went up to feel for the man's pulse, and came back to where I was watching.

"There is no sign of life in him at all," Dorantes told me. I could see that the man's face was bloodless and he lay without breathing, without moving at all.

The people started to cover the man with a mat.

"No," instructed Núñez, "leave off the mat." Suddenly, Núñez seemed filled with new life. He stood over the lifeless man and slowly made the sign of the cross. Then he lifted his eyes upward and in a loud voice, in Spanish, prayed, *"Bendito Dios,* Giver of Life, restore life to this man and give him back his strength and health." Then he lowered his head and in a low, but audible voice, I heard him say the prayer that he always used, which he called *"El Padre Nuestro"* (Our Father). By now I had learned this prayer by memory, and whispered it along with Núñez.

Then he instructed the villagers, "Leave this man uncovered." The sun was shining brightly and I could see the deathly pallor of the man's face as the sun shone on it.

Now the Susolos began bringing many sick people to Núñez for treatment, and he prayed over them and made the sign of the cross and blew on them, one at a time. Several of these had complained of constant dizziness before his treatment. I took note of every case and each individual face.

When Núñez had finished, the Susolos brought him a large basket of ripe tunas. He ate two or three of the tunas and divided the rest among those of us who had come with him.

Núñez and Dorantes set off to return to the Avavares while the rest of us remained with the Susolos. I stayed because I wanted to see how all the sick people felt who had been treated. And especially I kept watching the man whom everybody had thought dead, as he lay with his face exposed to the afternoon sun.

A cluster of villagers gathered around each person who had been treated. Each one I observed said he was well, and most had started moving around normally. It was hard for me to believe, yet I forced myself to accept what my eyes were seeing.

Late in the afternoon, a shout went up from the handful of people who were close to the man thought to be dead. I hurried over to see him and noticed that his body was moving. I saw his eyelids flutter and close, flutter again and open wide. A shout went up from the onlookers, and people from all over the village came hurrying up to see what was going on. The man moved his arms and legs. He sat up, looking bewildered. Then I saw him stand and start to walk. A great shout went up from the people and, without realizing it, I found myself shouting, too.

"Food," said the revived man. "I need food. I am weak." They brought him cooked venison and tunas, which he ate slowly. He went in the direction of his lodge, which had been torn down.

"My lodge," he said. "Where is my lodge?"

"It was torn down."

"Torn down? That happens only when a man dies."

"You were dead," he was told by a friend. "Your heart had stopped beating. You had no pulse. You were not breathing. Your eyes turned backward in death. The Child of the Sun asked the Great Spirit to bring you back to life and restore your health. That is why you are alive! Come stay with me tonight."

As we returned to the Avavares the next morning, we could talk of nothing but the unusual restoration of life to the man who had died. I went immediately to Núñez to give him an eyewitness account of what had happened.

When he heard it he exclaimed, *"Gracias a Dios!"* (Thanks be to God!)

Had I seen a man raised from the dead? I do not know. Even if he had not been dead, he had been sick enough for everyone to believe he was dead. Something very unusual had evidently happened to him. His sickness had disappeared and he had started moving, walking around, eating and acting perfectly normal.

That night I went to Núñez. "Was that man really dead, Master?"

"Quien sabe?" he answered. "If he was, he is alive now. If he was sick, he was very sick, and is completely well now."

"Master, I have never heard of such a thing as a dead man being restored to life."

"I have! It happened long, long when Jesu-Cristo, a son of God, was on earth. He came to a village and found two of his friends, two sisters named Mary and Martha, mourning because their brother Lazarus had died. 'If you had been here he would not have died,' they said to him. So *el Cristo* went to the tomb, which was a cave with a rock closing its mouth. He said, 'Take away the stone from the mouth of the cave.'

"Martha said to him, 'Lord, by this time he stinketh, because he has been dead four days.' But the people moved the stone from the mouth of the cave. Jesus lifted his eyes upward and said, 'Father, I thank Thee that Thou has heard me. And I know that Thou hearest me always, but because of the people that stand by I said it, that they may believe that Thou hast sent me.' Then he cried with a loud voice, 'Lazarus, come forth.'

"And the man who had been dead came out of the cave, still bound in his burial clothes. Jesus said, 'Loose him and let him go.' And Lazarus, who had been dead was completely restored to life."

Núñez was shedding tears at the end of the story. Finally he said, "Jesus told his disciples, 'The works that I do shall ye do; and greater works than these, because I go to my Father.'"

Núñez said to me, "Whatever happened to that man whom everyone thought dead was something wonderful that God did."

"How do you do these things, Master?"-

"Like I said, it was God who did it, not I. I am only His servant who prays to Him and tries to do His will. The question is asked in the scripture: 'Is anything too hard for God?' And in another place the answer is given: 'Nothing is too hard for God!'"

That night, after I had spread my buffalo robes under the stars in solitude, I lay awake a long time, remembering everything that had happened that day. These things which I had heard of as I traveled, I was now seeing with my own two eyes. What was this? Surely these men were from the Great Spirit.

. . . Being alone much of the time, I had ample opportunity to think. Lying awake at night under the stars in the sky, watching the red ball of the sun arise from the rim of the world in the morning and shed its golden light upon the world, I had thought much about the Great Spirit who had created all.

Sometimes I would think how I had been made different from other men. And bitterly I would say to the Great Spirit, "Why did You do this to me? It is not fair that I am made as I am." Now was the Great Spirit showing me how He cares for all men and wishes to heal the sick, if only we believe in Him? I would finally sleep without an answer to these questions. . .

When I awakened in the early morning I took in the fresh smell of the cedars in the damp, cool air. As the sun came up, the dew was sparkling everywhere. It was a glistening world, a fresh world that seemed new and wonderful to me.

Chapter VII

A Change in My Thinking

According to Núñez's instructions, I looked for an opportunity to hear Dorantes' narrative of what happened to them before they escaped. I had become friends with these companions of Núñez as my Spanish improved. I knew that Núñez and his countrymen had all come across the ocean together, and that each Spaniard had become the slave of a different Indian family. I was sure that their lives had been full of trial and suffering before they escaped.

Shortly after my conversation with Núñez, one day I said to Dorantes, "I would like to hear everything that happened to you after you were separated from Núñez on *La Isla del Malhado.*"

He answered, "Cazador, one of these days when it rains and you are not able to hunt, come here to my lodge and I shall tell you the whole story."

On one such day, I made my way to Dorantes' lodge in the dripping rain. I had let Bolo out to hunt, since he did not mind rain, and he had returned with a fat rabbit which I brought with me. Dorantes was grateful for this fresh meat and, since I had already skinned and cleaned the animal, he began to cook it at once.

"Now for the story of what happened to us after we left the

Island of Bad Luck." Dorantes then told me all that happened to them before they finally rejoined Núñez. It was a tale of servitude. As slaves of Indian families, they had been punished frequently and ridiculed. Dorantes told me all this in great detail. Later I also read the account in Núñez's journal . . .

As I mentioned earlier, after I had been with the Avavares about a week, I noticed an older woman acting in a friendly way to me. Her name was Akka and I think she was middleaged. Yet she had a strong, healthy body, and great kindness in her face.

She told me once, "I am a widow, Cazador. Five years ago my husband, who was the finest man in the village, was killed by an arrow. Not a man in the village can compare with my husband. So I have not found another husband, but live alone in my lodge.

"I had a daughter who married a good man in a village about two days' journey from here. My one son left this village two years ago, and I do not know where he is. I need you as a son, Cazador. I like you and would like to care for you in every way I can."

Of course, I thought of my own mother and her love for me. But I remembered also that she had been ashamed of me. Tears came to my eyes as I recalled my great disappointment when I realized my mother was ashamed of me.

Akka had the feeling of a mother for me, but without any shame. So I welcomed her motherly love and tenderness for me. It was something I needed more than I had known. I went to her lodge often to eat and visit with her.

One day I told her, "You do not treat me as other women do. They think I am strange because I am a dwarf. You do not seem to notice my size or, if you do, it seems to make no difference."

"I am not blind," answered Akka. "Of course I know you are a dwarf. But it is not a man's size that counts. It is his spirit. I can feel that you are a good person. You are friendly and kind and honest. That your legs did not grow long makes no difference at all to me. I know many men that are tall. Some of them are also very stupid. Some are not likeable at all.

"Another thing, Cazador—you are good at everything you do. You are better than any hunter I know. You deserve the name the Spaniards gave you, Cazador. You are clever with your hands, also."

It was good to hear Akka say these things. I felt she accepted me just as I was, that she respected me and liked me. This role of an honored, favored son was one I liked a great deal. Nevertheless, I said to her, "Most women will have nothing to do with me. No woman in any Pueblo village would ever consider me as a husband even though my father offered any family whose daughter married me a fortune in turquoise. This made me feel left out and unwanted. Even my own mother and older sisters were ashamed of me. This made me bitter. Why would the Great Spirit make me this way so that I belonged to no one?"

"Who can question the ways of the Great Spirit? He has many purposes and many ways, but I have always felt that all His ways, even if I did not understand them, were best for us."

I knew that I, too, thought this way. And in a flash there came to me a new understanding.

"Akka, what you say is true, very true. And suddenly I have seen the great purpose or a part of it. You see, if I had not been a dwarf, I would never have known the healer, my teacher and my leader. Nothing has ever come to me that was as important as knowing this man. My village lies far to the north and Núñez will never go there. I would rather be a dwarf and know Núñez than be a man tall and handsome and not know him." I was shedding tears as I spoke my new understanding. Akka came to me, stroked my head, and laid her hand on my shoulder. I knew I respected and admired Núñez, but this awareness of how important he was in my life was sudden and powerful.

"Yes, I see this, Cazador. You are right."

Akka delighted in cooking for me and feeding me from her hidden stores of nuts and dried tunas. I caught so much small game with Bolo's skilled help that I kept Akka supplied with meat. So our friendship and companionship grew stronger and was good for both us.

Núñez met me one day day and said, "Cazador, I am concerned about the way Estevánico behaves. It is understandable that he should seek the favors of the unmarried girls. But it is hard to understand that he must want so many of the married women. Their husbands are angry. I must warn Estevánico that there will be violence if he continues to go after the married women."

Of course, I had noticed this and had seen the scowls on the faces of the husbands. One day Estevánico ran panting from the woods. "*Maestro,* I almost got killed. As I was walking in the woods, an arrow whistled by my ear and stuck quivering in a tree nearby. It would have killed me if it had hit a vital spot! You must speak to the village about this, *Maestro!*"

"I shall speak to no one but you, Estevánico. I have talked to you about trying to get the favors of the married women. Their husbands are warning you. If you want to get yourself killed, keep on as you are, and gain the enmity of all the married men. If you will leave the married women alone, I think you will have no more trouble."

Estevánico heeded Núñez and received no more threatening warnings. The Avavares felt complimented if their unmarried daughters were sought after by the Spaniards, since they felt the Spaniards came from heaven and were like gods. Both Dorantes and Castillo were favored by desirable unmarried women. Estevánico continued seeking any favors that came his way.

Núñez, however, was the busiest of all the Spaniards. After the restoration of the dead man in the Susolo village, Núñez's fame as a miracle worker spread to faraway villages and Indians came on long journeys, sometimes carrying the sick on stretchers made of woven fibers extended between strong poles. When he was not healing, he was teaching me. With the hours of his day so full, he paid little attention to the available Indian girls.

Yet, of all the unmarried young girls of the village, the most desirable had eyes only for Núñez. She was a tall girl, graceful and strong. She did him as many favors as she could and, although it was clear to me that she had affection for Núñez and only him, he seemed almost unaware of her. She was called Unla and was well liked by the whole village.

I was close to Núñez's lodge the day she brought him a well-made pair of moccasins, beautifully beaded. She laid them at his feet and looked up at him. From where I was standing I could see her large, dark eyes clearly, and it seemed to me she almost worshiped him. Núñez was very grateful and laid his hand on her head, and I could see his lips moving in prayer as he touched her.

I came slowly to know Unla. I think she wanted my friendship because she knew that I was taking lessons from Núñez, and that he was my friend. One sunny morning as I walked through the many lodges, all made of woven mats, I became aware of Unla walking by me.

"Those were beautiful moccasins you gave Núñez," I told her.

"Yes, I wanted them to be beautiful for him. And I hope they will serve him a long time."

"He needed them. His old ones were worn and soiled and the bottoms were nearly gone."

"He is a great man. When he touched my head, it seemed that life was flowing through me. I never had that feeling at any time in my life. Before he came to our village, I would not have believed that such a man had ever lived. He is like no one else on earth."

Of course, I thought just as she did. And I realized then the look of worship I had seen in her eyes had really been there!

I knew that Unla wove two thick mats for Núñez to sleep on. I did not know if she had ever shared them with him. If she had, I think I would have heard, because such things were common talk around the village.

Núñez made trips to neighboring villages whenever he was needed, and that was often. Every time he left, I would see Unla gazing after him and she would remain restless until he returned. She frequently came out of her lodge and gazed in the direction from which he would come. When he appeared, she was satisfied and would return to her lodge.

One of those days while she stood looking in the direction from which he would come, I joined her.

"You really miss him, don't you, Unla?"

"Yes," she answered simply. "I don't want him ever to leave, somehow. He is making my whole life different. Maybe it is because the Great Spirit seems so much more real to me and because I think this man knows the Great Spirit. If he didn't, how could he cure the sick? And why do I always feel so uplifted when he is around? Do you know what all the people are saying?''

"I may not have heard what you have."

"They are saying as long as he is with us, we shall never die."

"No, I have never heard that."

"Do you believe this, Cazador?"

"I don't know what I believe, Unla. All I know is that Núñez has changed my life, just as he has yours. I can never be the same. The way I look at everything is different. People are different. The sky is different, the stars are different. So are the trees and the grass. And I am no longer bitter."

"Bitter? What do you mean, bitter?" She looked at me baffled.

"I resented being a dwarf. I felt the Great Spirit was unjust to make me as I am. And then I understood if I had not been a dwarf I would never have known Núñez because I lived far, far to the north where Núñez would never have gone. I became a trader because none of the women of my village would have me as a husband. And as a trader I wandered to the south where I met Núñez."

Unla said nothing. I was fond of her and found her a most desirable person. Yet I had to be realistic. Unla had heart only for Núñez. And even the most favored of the young men of the Avavares were not then in her thoughts. Her thoughts were for one man alone, and he was almost as unattainable as the sun whose child he was.

Then she said, "I think he is not of this earth. That is why he works such wonders."

"He says he is of the world, and that he came from a far land in a big canoe that held many men. He tells me they crossed a great lake of water so big that for days they traveled westward without seeing any land at all."

"I cannot understand that."

"Nor could I, at first. But as a trader I went to an island and stood on a smooth, sandy beach and saw water as far as the eye could see."

"His companions who are like him except for the big, dark one must have come from the same land; yet they are not like him."

One day in his teaching, Núñez told me, "Cazador, I have told you many things about our religion. I would like to bring them all together, so you have a clear picture of what we believe."

"This I would like, Núñez."

"First, let me say you are becoming a learned man. I have never known anyone to learn as fast as you. So the knowledge of our religion will be a part of your learning.

"Just as you say your people believe in the Great Spirit, my people believe that the stars, the moon, and the sun were created by the one whom we call *Dios*. All plants, all animals, the seas, the land, the mountains and plain are the work of His mind and His hands. Men and women everywhere are His handiwork, too.

"Many centuries ago—more than 1400 years ago—*Dios* sent His son to the earth. He was born as a baby to a beautiful mother named *Maria*. She was a virgin, even though she was giving birth to a baby."

"A virgin? How could that be?"

"The story says that God alone was the father of the baby, and the woman's husband, *José*, knew this and was not jealous. Later a number of other children were born to them.

"Even as a boy, Jesu-Cristo was noticed as being favored by God. When he grew to be a man he started teaching. He chose twelve men to go around with him and learn from him. He taught people that *Dios* was their Father and loved them. He also went around from village to village, healing the sick."

"You are like him, Master! You think only of helping all people. You heal the sick. You teach that *Dios* is our Father and loves us and wants us to do only that which is right."

"It is true I have patterned my life after his. But there were in that land evil men who, for no good reason, wanted to put Jesu-Cristo to death.

"They had a cruel way of making people die. They made big timbers and crossed them and nailed a man to that cross. So even though Jesu-Cristo had done no wrong, he was condemned to die on the cross. They nailed him to it, and put a crown of thorns on his head. So he died without hating those who killed him, showing God's great love for all men.

"They put him in a cave as a grave and, as their custom was, rolled a great stone to seal the mouth of the cave. But, wonderful to relate, on the third day, the great stone had been rolled away and an angel stood guard at the mouth of the cave. He said to the women who came to the cave, 'He is not here! He is risen from the dead!'

"Following this, Jesu-Cristo met with many of his disciples and taught and comforted them and told them to go out and teach and preach about him and his way of life. So we believe Jesu-Cristo was God's son and that only through him can men be saved."

"Only through him?"

"Yes! Only through him."

"But the Great Spirit shows Himself to all peoples. He has those who obey Him and believe in Him among all the tribes that I know."

"Yes, that is hard to understand. I just teach the mercy and the grace of God and do not puzzle much about these other hard questions."

"It is a wonderful story, and I know if this Jesu-Cristo walked among us, I would like him and want him to teach me."

When I saw Unla again I told her the complete story as Núñez had told it to me.

"The cross is the magic sign they make as they pray over the sick. I understand it better now," she said. "This story of Jesu-Cristo is a strange and wonderful story. And as you say, Núñez is like him. Núñez is the son of the Great Spirit."

"I, too, think this is true."

"And the way he was raised from the dead I would never have believed before. But after Núñez raised the dead man of the Susolos to life, I can believe that Jesu-Cristo was raised from the dead."

"Núñez says that now Jesu-Cristo's spirit lives above and anyone who wishes to have his spirit will receive it."

"Certainly Núñez has received his spirit."

Of all the village women of the Avavares only Unla and Akka were the ones I knew well. The language of the Avavares I spoke easily because it was so like my own tongue and like that of the Chorrucas.

None of these southern people could compare with my people of the Pueblos. My people all lived in permanent villages with

houses several stories high. They stored food for the cold months.
They domesticated the wild turkey. They were also skilled
hunters, killing many deer and, in season, many buffalo.

These Avavares were much inferior to my people. My people
wore beautiful clothes, both of cotton and deerskin. My people
wore moccasins. These men wore no clothes, many times even
when it was cold, and usually they would go barefoot. The
women were scantily covered with Spanish moss that grew from
the oaks. Not even Núñez wore clothes, nor Dorantes, nor
Castillo, nor Estevánico. Núñez said he grew accustomed to this
way of dressing when he first lived with the coastal Indians. Of
course, the Spaniards and the men of the Avavares all wore
breechclouts.

The Avavares, as I said before, were poor hunters. They killed
a few deer and caught a few fish, but killing deer required hard
work and long hours of stealthiness and skill which the
Avavares did not have. They wanted the easy food, fruit and
nuts, the red agarita berries, the dark wild persimmons and, of
course, the tuna. Many times they would go hungry, because
they had avoided the long hours and hard work of the hunt.

I became familiar with one of their men who was far better
than the others at killing deer. His name was Niggal. He had
observed my skill at getting meat and was particularly interested in my successful snares for small animals.

One day I asked him, "Niggal, why do you not plant corn, and
beans, and squash? This is what my people do. They never go
hungry."

He answered, "I have heard of people who do this thing. But
if we did, we could not move from place to place to where the
fruit ripens. We like to make our lodges where there is fruit."

"But sometimes fruit may be hard to find, as it is now that all
the nuts have been picked."

"That is true," he said. "Many times food is hard to get."

"If you planted corn in the good land and stored it, you would
never be hungry."

"That is not the way of the Avavares." This was all he said.
And I was no reformer, so I did not discuss it with him again. He
was not interested in doing anything that would help them live

better.

There was a shrub called mountain laurel growing in the hills. It bore beans that were bright red with a black spot. These beans were very hard. I had the idea that if I could make a hole through this hard bean, I could string a number of them on sinews spliced together and make an attractive string of beads. I first tried an awl made of flint, but it was very hard to make a hole this way. So I gave up that method.

Next I took a sharp metal arrowhead that I had acquired and heated it red-hot in the coals of a fire. I discovered this was the way to make a good hole through the bean. Also the dark, burned edges of the hole made a good contrast with the bright red of the bean. I found I could do this even as I took lessons from Núñez. It was slow work, but finally I had strung together about forty of the beads.

Núñez had been interested in this. When he saw my finished beads, he said, "They are very pretty. Are you going to wear them?"

I shook my head. "They are for Akka. She is a mother to me and I wish to show her my liking for her and my gratitude."

Akka was pleased with my gift and wore them all the time. Other women admired them and tried to get me to make more. Finally I made another string, but put it away with my other trading goods.

Chapter VIII
Núñez Tells Me
How He Became
a Child of the Sun

One reason I had come south was because the winters were not as cold. Rarely was there snow and ice. Only once during this winter with the Avavares was there either snow or much ice. It stayed on the ground only two days before it was melted by the warm sun.

Even in the winter on the good days I went fishing at the place where there was a bluff over the river and large rocks below. Many rattlesnakes would come out and warm themselves on these rocks. Now in the cold weather they were in their dens, hibernating. Usually, I cooked my fish and ate them where I caught them before returning to the village. With all the hunger there, I felt that seeing me with fish would produce envy among the villagers and I wanted to keep their goodwill.

Akka was so good to me and such a nice person that I smuggled fish into her lodge usually after dark. If her people had known she had fish, they would have come to her lodge demanding some.

Akka was interested in Núñez just as Unla was, but perhaps for different reasons. She was unlike Unla, who was a very young woman with a great desire for men. I told Akka the entire story of Jesu-Cristo as Núñez had told it to me. She was fascinated by it and, like Unla, said, "Núñez is like this son of the Great Spirit. This helps me to understand him better."

Akka believed in storing food, such as nuts and dried tunas. She concealed these places well, knowing the perpetual hunger of her people. She always shared food with me as I did with her. One evening while we were eating together she mentioned that her married daughter, Aina, had asked Akka to come to her village two days' journey away and live with her.

"I like her and her husband. So I may move to her village when warm weather comes. I like her four children."

Akka was good for me. I felt loved and respected and wanted. I can never forget this fine person and what she did for me. I talked to her freely of what I had heard of Muna and how I was going to the far western country in search of her. She listened with interest and accepted this.

That winter was the best time I had ever had. When the days were cold with the wind blowing its icy blasts, we stayed in our lodges and I spent many hours learning Spanish and talking with the Spaniards. I listened carefully to their speech and tried to speak as they did. I asked many questions and practiced my writing.

One day in the middle of winter, the southwest wind was blowing and it became as warm as spring. I was about to go hunting with Bolo when Núñez came up to me and said, "Let me go with you; I have something I wish to tell you. I think you will understand it better than anyone I know."

That day Bolo hunted well, bringing us several rabbits and a young raccoon. Núñez and I sat on rocks by a clear spring flowing with great volume. "You see, Cazador," he began, "I was trained from my youth as a soldier. I learned the art of warfare and killing and how to fight battles. I fought in a war in Italy and killed many of the enemy. I was told I was a hero but I knew it was not true. I was told it was patriotic to kill for my country. But even then I knew it was wrong, very wrong. It was against the law of God.

"Because I had earned a good reputation as a soldier, this evil man, Pánfilo Narvaez, chose me to be second in command of his expedition. When you asked me why I would follow such a selfish, horrible man, I told you that it was because I felt it was my destiny, Perhaps it was; we shall see.

"The Spaniards have always been cruel to the Indians, making slaves of them to work in the mines or to dive for pearls, or to do killing hours of labor on the *haciendas* To my people, the Indians were like cattle or horses, except they were not treated as kindly. Some of our soldiers slaughtered the Indians for sport, as a game, if you can imagine such savagery!

"When Narvaez was a soldier in Cuba, he watched while his men beheaded the men, women, and children of the Indian villages. He was a child of Satan. I could never have been as cruel to the Indians as Narvaez and his soldiers, but my attitude toward them was wrong because I still thought them the same as animals, to be used for our pleasure and profit.

"A *padre* by the name of Las Casas had returned to Spain from Cuba and told his story. He was a priest of the church who had owned Indian slaves. And one day he had the knowledge given him that his holding of slaves was against the will of God. His eyes were opened that God wanted the Indians treated well, as dignified human beings rather than animals.

"So Las Casas set free all his own slaves and tried without success to get others in Cuba to free their Indian slaves. Las Casas returned to Spain, boldly telling about the atrocities of the Spaniards toward the Indians. Charles the Fifth, our ruler, listened to him and agreed with him and issued orders for all the Indians to be treated well. Charles, the emperor, is a man of goodwill.

"Cazador, I understood clearly what Las Casas was talking about. But, being trained as a soldier in killing, I still felt it was our right to take the Indians' wealth, their women, and, if we wanted, their lives. I still felt that we had the right to make them slaves; I was still hard and cold and, like most Spaniards, I ridiculed Las Casas' ideas.

"Then I was shipwrecked on the Island of Ill Fate. And it was the Indians who fed us and gave us shelter. These were the worst of the Indians, those of the coast and the islands. They saved our lives. I saw that even these barbarous Indians were people. As bad as they were, they treated their children kindly. They were human with a certain amount of goodness in them. And they saved our lives, as I said.

"After our boat overturned we swam to shore and built up our fires. Bereft of everything and stark naked in the cold, I felt that I was simply receiving what I had been giving—misery and heartache.

"The Indians fed us and took us to their homes. We became their slaves, and I knew for the first time in my life what it was like to be a slave and belong to others like any lifeless property. I knew what it was like to have to obey hard masters, whether I was sick or well, hungry or weak or thirsty.

"I knew what was happening to me, Cazador. God was showing me what I had done to others, or wanted to do to them. I was being humbled and shown how wrong was my attitude, not only toward the Indians, but toward all my fellow beings.

"I had been selfish, and hard, and cold. I had been inhuman. God was showing me a picture of how I had been, and it was an ugly picture.

"I worked for my Indian family from early daylight until after dark. I dug roots until my hands were raw and bleeding. Through becoming a slave, I saw how wrong I had been and how heartless against God and His created children."

Núñez sat down on a log and I saw him put his head in his hands and sob.

"I was so wrong, Cazador! Las Casas, the man of God, was so right! When I was humbled and enslaved and brought low, at last I could see it.

"Then I was forced, as I told you, into the work of a healer. Again it was God showing me how I could change and how I could help people, rather than hurt them. Little by little, my heart got right with God and my fellow man! And I began to understand the spirit of Jesu-Cristo.

"When I escaped, I had arrived at the place where all I wanted to do was to be of help to others. God showed me, through the healing work I was doing, how much He loved the Indians. Now I want nothing from anybody but their love. Now I want only to help, not only the Indians, but everybody. I wanted them to know God through faith. I wanted them healed of sickness and suffering, through faith. One time Jesu-Cristo said, 'I am come that ye might have life and have it more abundantly.' This is what I want now for all the earth's people. Finally, I have become God's man and now I want only to do His work.''

This was the outpouring of feeling and thought that I, Cazador, heard that beautiful, mild winter day. I saw that the Great Spirit had worked to change Núñez as He was also shaping my life to change me. And as I sat there, silent after hearing Núñez's heartbroken confession, I think I knew for the first time how much the Great Spirit loved us all.

Núñez had to return to the village. I gave him the young raccoon and two rabbits, and I stayed under the big cottonwood on the rocky edge of the clear, cold spring. Bolo was far away, ranging the woods, searching for game. The mild southwest wind was blowing small, light clouds across the sky. There were leafless mesquite trees nearby and the wind whispered against their thorny branches. As I sat there, I felt a presence so real, so wonderful that my mind was filled with awe and worship.

Chapter IX

The Child of the Sun
Starts His Long Journey
Northwest

My friendship with Akka was good. She admired me and was proud of me, and I could feel this when we were together. She had adopted me as a son.

One day she said to me, "You see, I like to be with you because you think well and talk well. Then you are a beautiful person to look at. The goodness of your face comes from deep within you."

Later she said, "If you will go with me to the village where my daughter lives, I would like to have you live in my lodge all the time. I would like for you to be my husband. I know that you are much younger than I. The people of the village will ridicule me at first and say that I have stolen someone's little boy to be my husband. But I know that you are more of a man than any Indian I know. Eventually the people will forget this and we can have a happy life together. I know you feel that your path points with Núñez to the far west. If this is what is best for you, although I shall be saddened by your leaving, I still want you to go."

At first I could hardly believe my ears. I, Cazador, the dwarf, was desired by a fine woman to be her husband. Akka's kind words moved me so much that at first I could not answer, but only sat with tears in my eyes. Akka was the most loving and understanding woman I had ever met. Now she reached over with her fingers and lightly stroked my cheek.

At last, when I could speak, I told her, "Akka, you are a beautiful person. I love you. You have given me something I can never forget, and shall always remember with thanksgiving."

"You are not to answer now," she said. "Think on it, and if it seems the best way to you, I shall be made happy. But if your life is to go with Núñez, I shall understand."

One day not long after this, Akka said, "Cazador, I know that you feel your littleness, but do you realize that everyone I know feels little in one way or another? Remember that your are big in courage and skill, and in your great goodness. This is the way I see you."

For many days my heart was singing with joy, that such a wonderful thing had happened to me. Yet I knew I must journey to the west with Núñez and search for Muna, who was to me like a dream in the night.

Those eight months in the village of the Avavares were the beginning of a new life for me. I no longer felt fettered by my smallness. I was no longer ashamed of being a dwarf. The bitterness with which I had lived for years had vanished almost as if it had never existed. I knew I was desirable as a man and a husband. Some day I would have my own home, my own wife and children and I would find my rightful place in life. I was filled with courage and with joy. For the first time in many years, I had a feeling of wholeness and well being. Now I knew I would not always be a trader, but would find a place of greater usefulness and service.

The days began growing longer and warmer. Most of the ducks and geese had flown north. Only a few flocks were left. Now that the water was warmer, I planned a surprise for Núñez.

I found a hollow log and built a fire under it about three feet from the end. When the bottom had burned through, I turned it over and burned through the upper half. Then I burned a big hole in the bottom of the log; next I scraped all the burnt wood away from around the edge of the big hole. Now I tried it to see if my head would go through the hole. It would, so I was satisfied.

I did this close to a small lagoon where about twenty ducks were swimming on the water. The males had green heads with a stripe around the neck and the females were brown.

I rolled my log-section to some brush cover at one end of the lagoon, and slid the log into the water. I slipped out of my deerskin clothes and moccasins, and dove naked into the water, gasping from the coldness of it. I stuck my head through the hole I had made in the log and paddled slowly toward the ducks. Finally, I was among them. They were feeding below the surface, ducking their heads down and leaving their tails above the water. As a duck moved into this position, I would grab it by the head and quietly pull it under. I tied each drowned duck below the log with a long sinew around my waist. I was able to catch about ten of the ducks before the others became alarmed and flew away.

How Núñez and I feasted on those ducks! I also took Akka a fat hen-duck, after darkness as usual. We ate the duck together in her lodge. After we had eaten, she said to me, "I now know what you must do. You do not have to tell me. I wish for you only the greatest happiness in all you do. The beauty of your life has blessed and helped me. I shall remember it always and my memory of our friendship will make me happy."

In this way Akka set me free to travel the long trail ahead of me. But best of all, she had freed my spirit from its burden of bitterness, and given me a new self-respect.

Spring had come. The leaves of the mesquite trees unfurled in light, fresh green that was a feast to the eyes. The nut trees also budded and put on new leaves. The Avavares said when these two things happened there would be no more cold weather.

There were other signs of spring. The scissortails made merry as they flew from tree to tree and upward in the air, singing. They had come back from the far south. At night I listened and heard the first whippoorwills, as they, too, announced their return from the far south. Most of the robins, who had wintered with us, were now gone.

Núñez suddenly decided to go north and, with Dorantes, Castillo and Estevánico, silently and secretly left the Avavares in the dark very early one morning. The Avavares, of course, did not want him to go and, had they known he was leaving, might have delayed him several days.

As Núñez had told me where I could find him, I set off to other villages not far from his northwest route to do some trading. My departure from Akka was sad, but each of us knew that my place lay with Núñez on the trail toward the far west.

Akka had given me what I clearly needed, abundant love and acceptance. And she had paid me the final tribute of wanting me to live in her lodge permanently. It was Akka more than anyone else who had taken away my bitterness about being a dwarf. Now I knew that being a dwarf could never keep me from living a full, happy life. The great love she had for me had freed me. And therefore along with my sadness at parting from her was joy as I faced the future. I had a new confidence, a new respect and liking for myself.

I thought much about this as I started my solitary trip away from her forever. I spent my nights in the open. I saw the great swarms of stars fade overhead and the light in the east grow stronger. I did my trading quickly in the several villages I visited.

When I joined Núñez again, he told me, "We went to do our healing work among the Arbadaos. They are a poor and shiftless people. We were hungry all the time. They killed a few deer and I asked to scrape the skins because I could eat of those scrapings. Whenever we were lucky enough to have meat, we found that if we began to cook it, the Arbadaos would snatch it away from us. So as much as I dislike to, I ate my meat raw."

I was glad I had not been with Núñez when he went to the village of the Arbadaos. But it showed me again that this man would go to any length to help people, no matter how wretched they were. Indeed, when the Spaniards took up their northwestern journey again, Núñez had only one thought—that was to help the people of all these villages. I, on the other hand, was impatient to travel as much as we could each day.

Many times as I went to sleep, I could clearly see the face of my loving Akka. How I wished I could see her again. But I knew this was all behind me. Then I would think of Muna far, far to the west. I would try to picture her, but I could not. I knew she was small like me—a dwarf. The traveler had said she was pretty and that no man wanted her for a wife. These thoughts made me impatient, particularly when the Spaniards would stay in a village several days. Gradually we continued north, following the River of Nuts, and then its bend toward the west. This was the way I wanted to go. I felt my destiny was in this direction; that I would find Muna, and would have a wife of my own and a lodge of my own.

The natives of this country knew certain plants, whose leaves they dried. These they would mix with the dried powder of a small cactus, the peyote. They claimed that the smoke from this cactus mixture in their pipes gave them visions. They saw beautiful colors. The ground which is always still began to move like water when they smoked this. They would give anything they had for this mixture to smoke.

This was the time when the agarita berries on certain thorny bushes were bright red and ripe and ready to eat. I would put the cured hide of a deer under one side of an agarita bush and beat that side with a stick. The berries fell thickly on my deerskin and were sweet and tart to my taste. Also the beans of the mesquite trees could be ground into powder and eaten. Some of the tribes mixed this powder with earth—to make it taste better, they said, although I did not like the idea of eating dirt.

Every morning the Spaniards would kneel, make the sign of the cross, and talk to the Great Spirit. They did this at night, too, before they slept.

Since coming to know Núñez my idea of the Great Spirit had changed. There was a time when I knew there was such a Spirit who had made the stars, the rivers, the clouds, all the animals and all men. I knew this. But He seemed far, far away. Now I began to feel He was near. I felt that He was with me somehow, in my mind and my heart. I felt that He had used Núñez to teach me these things.

Núñez talked to me freely one night. He said, "Cazador, I do not like something these Indians have started doing."

"You mean their plundering every village?"

"Yes, that is wrong and yet I have no power to stop them. Oh, I have tried to stop them, but they say, 'Well, Child of Heaven, if we plunder the village we come to, the people can make it up by plundering the next village they go to when they follow you.' I don't like this and I am praying it will stop."

One reason that the Indians came to believe in the Spaniards was because they wanted nothing for themselves. If they were given gifts, they gave them back to others who needed them. I suggested to Núñez that if the messengers that always went before him would tell the people of each village to hide their goods, it might stop the plundering. But this failed and the pillaging continued.

Núñez and those of us with him traveled on. We were being guided by women from another village. Soon, we reached a large, clear spring and drank from it with pleasure. We bathed in the small, cool river below the spring. Then the women guided us across a larger river to a village of over a hundred lodges, which we reached at sunset. Messengers had been ahead of us and the excitement of the people of this village, in anticipation of Núñez's arrival, was the greatest I have ever seen.

All the people came to meet us, shouting in loud voices. Many of them were shaking gourds filled with pebbles which they considered sacred objects. The people were dancing wildly, slapping their thighs. They crowded around Núñez, each trying to touch him. He was pressed from every side. Finally, he and the other Spaniards were taken to their lodges.

The people stayed up all night feasting and dancing. I left the village and spread out my buffalo robes far away where the noise would not keep me awake. Bolo was all the company I needed right then.

The next day everyone in the village wanted to be touched by Núñez and, as usual, they brought him their sick, over whom he made the sign of the cross and prayed. They believed that Núñez was a god come down to earth and that they were greatly favored that he walked among them.

Chapter X

The Child of the Sun
Becomes a Surgeon
with Primitive Instruments

One day we entered a village of people who were strongly and beautifully built. Their skins were very light, like my own and my people. It seemed to me that all the women I saw were well formed, graceful with attractive faces. But among these fine people there were many sick ones, over whom Núñez made the sign of the cross and prayed. And it seemed that many were cured.

In my journeying, as I said before, I had long ago learned to trot along with Bolo. That way, in spite of my short legs, I could cover many leagues in a day. I now knew the direction of our travel as we followed the river that flowed northwest. Since the noise and hubbub of the excited throngs around Núñez bothered me, I always started early and stayed several miles ahead. One day, as I came to a rise in the ground, it seemed that I could see a blue cloud on the horizon. Then I saw it was not moving, and I knew that these were high mountains. Gradually, as I trotted along the trail, the mountains grew larger to my eyes. Finally I saw

that there were also mountains to the southwest.* This looked
good to me, since we were approaching a different kind of
country and I knew we were making progress toward my goal.
Also we were drawing closer to my homeland. It had been many
years since I had seen high mountains, and the sight of them
gave me a good feeling.

The Indians called this the River of Bitter water,** and
because of its bad taste they did not drink it. Creeks ran into the
River of Bitter Water and always fresh good water was available
if I reached it well before the crowds—which I made sure to do
since I could no longer talk much to the Spaniards and found the
clamor about them too noisy. They now usually spoke only
among themselves, and not much to their Indian followers. Since
the languages were no longer understood by any of us, we used
the sign language when we needed to communicate.

On my travel alone up the Bitter Water, I had much time to
think. Many things that Akka had told me continued to come
back to me. Her one comment that I remembered most was that
every person, no matter how big he was, felt little in some ways,
and that it was not the size of the person that counted, but his
spirit.

So I told myself, "That I am a dwarf is nothing for me to be
ashamed of. If I like people, either men or women, I shall show
my liking, without shame or fear, and I shall receive friendship
from those who are supposed to be my friends." As I thought
about this, my confidence grew. I felt everything was going to be
better for me, since now I had inner courage and strength.

Núñez and his companions spent each night in some village
not far from the river, and I continued ahead of the crowds. Each
day I watched the mountains grow larger. One high mountain ***
at the south end of the range we were closest to had sheer, steep
bluffs that rose up to great heights. I could see a darkness

---

  * These were the Davis Mountains.

 ** This was the Pecos River, also called by the Indians the River of The
    Buffalos.

*** Guadalupe Peak

high on the mountains that I knew to be pine trees, although I was too far to see any individual tree clearly. I watched these high rocky promontories with great pleasure.

Stretching away toward either side of the river were low shrubs. These were dark green greasewood shrubs, sage and low mesquite bushes. After a rain, even a small shower, I always liked the fresh, pungent odor of the greasewood. Also the sage bloomed periodically. It had lavender flowers, and where the sage was thick one could see a blanket of lavender. In one place I saw acres and acres of wild poppies in colorful fields reaching all the way to the foot of the mountains.

The plundering of each village the Indians came to would have greatly disturbed my trade had I not arrived in each village long before the multitudes following Núñez. During my eight months with the Avavares I had made many combs and these were in great demand. The first comb I had made after I came to know Akka was for her, because she loved to keep her hair clean, neatly combed and arranged. So, for her I made the best that I could. First I would form the proper length of wood by burning limbs of trees into sections each about as long (after the charred ends were scraped away) as the hand of a large man. These I split into slabs as flat as I could make them. The teeth of the comb had to run with the grain of the wood. These, too, I shaped by careful burning and scraping.

On my way south from my own village I had found in a village a spearhead of metal for which I had traded a turquoise stone. I had no idea where it came from or who found it or made it. I only knew it would be useful to me. I had carved from sandstone a holder for this piece of metal so that my hand would not burn when I held it. This was the arrow-point I used to help make the beads from laurel when I was with the Avavares. My well-made combs were my most desired item of trade.

I did not like my solitary life on this part of my journey. My family far to the north had been so affectionate. My mother and father and brothers and sisters had played with me and spoiled me and loved me. I did not like complete solitude.

My brothers, who were large and strong, always made me feel weak and unable to do much. This was true even before anyone knew that I would never grow to a normal height.

Of them all, only my father had treated me with the expectancy that I would become skilled and capable. He taught me lessons in tracking until I became unusually skillful at it. He taught me lessons of quick disappearance in timber and brush until I had well mastered that also. As a child I had learned the sign language so useful to me now.

Upon reaching the age when I should have grown tall and did not, most of my family and my whole tribe felt sorry for me that I would always be short and small. From about the age of 15 *años*, as the Spaniards call their twelve-month periods with their four seasons, I began to feel ashamed of myself because I was so small. This shame remained with me wherever I went. I left my village when, as the Spaniards say, I had 18 *años*. That was 8 years ago. . .a long time to carry a burden of shame. When Nalla accepted me and I made love to her and she told me how much she liked me, she helped me to feel better about myself. But, of course, her frank refusal to consider me as a possible husband, again made me feel inferior.

Naturally, I knew I had many skills and much knowledge, and that I learned easily and well. My father had also taught me skill with bow and arrows, but the bow had to be small enough for my size and strength, and this, too, reminded me that I was not as tall as other men. I carried a bow and arrows on my sledge and used them if I needed to; and sometimes, by careful stalking, I could get close enough to deer, both those of the brush and those of the plains. But my small bow just did not have the range of the longer, stronger bows.

Also, I knew I was well formed and strong for my size. My arms and legs were not extremely large but my muscles and sinews were strong and skillful. I knew my head, the largest part of my short body, was well formed and my face good to look on. I had seen my reflection many times in still pools. And different people had told me this, too. But this did not make up for the fact that I was and would always be a dwarf.

As I traveled alone, my mind went over all these things. I was not thinking logically, but accepting all thoughts that came to my mind. It was Akka who had really begun to change my attitude about my size. Her desire for me as a husband and her open invitation for me to become her husband were a great compliment. But her motherly love for me was the greatest boon, the knowledge that she respected me and accepted me as I was.

I thought repeatedly of her wisdom in telling me that everyone felt small about some things and that it was not a person's size but his spirit which really counted. This taught me so much, since now I knew I could have just as great and fine a spirit as anyone alive. It was this that had so much to do with losing all of my shame about myself.

Núñez's liking for me, his desire to teach me and befriend me, and the frequent talks we had opened a completely new life for me. His knowledge of the Great Spirit had also worked wonders with me. Perhaps this was the most important thing. For I came to understand that if I am made by the Great Spirit, then I am well made; and also I am a part of a great plan. And if the life that is in me is from the Great Spirit, then He sustains me and lives in me as He lives in all things. This knowledge taught me who I am and what I am.

While I had made many lonely journeys before, these present solitary days meant more than all others in clarifying my thinking, since I had more to build on. Now as I came to a new village, I was no longer ashamed. I knew the Great Spirit was in me, and this made me as large as the largest warrior, and with an inner strength as great as the strongest person.

As I entered a village, this good feeling about myself had an effect on the people I met. They treated me with a new respect. Also the young girls seemed to notice me more, and favorably so because they now smiled at me. But I missed the companionship with Akka and with Núñez, who now rarely had time to talk to anyone.

I had begun to question and wonder about Muna. Just because she was a dwarf like me did not mean she would like me, nor did it mean I would like her. How foolish of me to have thought that size alone would make that much difference! While Nalla would not consider me as a husband, I liked her because of her beauty both of spirit and of body; and this is what she liked about me, although my shortness kept her from considering me as a husband. My size had made all the difference with Nalla.

But size made no difference to Akka, who was the finest woman I had ever known. And Núñez, who was to me the greatest man on earth, had never seemed to be affected by my size. From that first day when he openly recognized I was a dwarf, he had treated me as a man whom he wanted for a friend; and later, as a man he respected and liked very much. So I had been blessed in many ways by the Great Spirit, Núñez's *Bendito Dios,* and I was thankful.

The high cliffs to the west had now begun to grow much smaller, and the range of the mountains they belonged to, much lower. But up to the northwest loomed another and greater mass, the Sacramento Mountains. The land had been gradually getting higher and the nights cooler, so that a buffalo robe with the hair turned in was needed for warmth. I became concerned about Núñez's comfort, for fear he had given away his buffalo robes as he was prone to giving away anything he had.

I therefore waited until the travelers overtook me and, when I had a moment alone with Núñez, asked him if he had buffalo robes to keep him warm. As I had suspected, he had only one left, but said he could be very comfortable rolled in this. I insisted that he take an extra robe, which I gave him. Estevánico, a giant by any standard, offered to carry both robes for him.

"We are turning west through the pass at the north end of these mountains," Núñez told me. "They say there are many villages among those mountains and many sick who need our help."

With this clear understanding of the route, once again I jogged on until I was far ahead of the noisy crowds that pressed around Núñez. I turned west on a well-traveled trail north of the Guadalupe Mountains and south of the larger Sacramento range that loomed ahead.

It was now much cooler with breezes sweeping down from the Sacramentos to the north. Each night after setting out my snares, I pulled great tufts of the plentiful grass and piled it under my buffalo robe. Then I heaped a mountain of grass over my top robe. This way I slept warm all night, even as I entered the higher mountains. Núñez's plan was to not climb to the highest part of this range, but only travel along the lower southern part of the elevation to serve the villages there.

The trail came to a village of many lodges, where I did much trading. Also, I found meat was now so plentiful that I set no snares, although Bolo, a lover of hunting, brought me fresh meat every day.

The next village I came to had heard that the great healer was coming. They led me to a man who had an arrowhead buried in his chest. He had been shot several years before. He and his family were hoping that Núñez could heal him. So I waited for Núñez, thinking of my long obsidian cutting tool which might be needed.

After I told him about the man and my obsidian knife, Núñez said, "Cazador, I'll remember that you have the tool if I need it."

"I keep it clean and well wrapped," I said. "Also, I have a bone needle and sinews for thread."

"Good!" he said.

It was about noon when Núñez arrived at the village. He went immediately to see the injured man. The sun was shining brightly and Núñez took him out in the sunlight to examine him. He made the sign of the cross and prayed as usual. He said he could feel the cartilage around the arrow under the skin.

He motioned all the Indians to stand back and give him room. He told Dorantes and Castillo, "Now keep them back. I need much light and plenty of room."

The wounded man lay prone on clean deerskins spread over a buffalo robe. Núñez made the sign of the cross again. I stood close by to help. He had me hand him the obsidian cutting tool. Without hesitation, Núñez began cutting the flesh over the wound. He used one of my bone needles to probe for the arrowhead. When he found the position of the arrowhead, he used the narrower end of the obsidian knife to pry it out.

Covered with blood, the long arrowhead eased out of the flesh. Then with the bone needle and sinews, Núñez drew the flesh of the wound together in two places. He washed off the blood and told the man's family to keep him lying in the sunlight until the

Namu probed for the arrowhead with the long bone needle.

blood of the wound clotted.

The chief of the village took the arrowhead and wiped it clean. Others examined it. The arrowhead passed from hand to hand. The Indians could talk of nothing but the skill of the great healer.

Chapter XI

The Child of the Sun
Turns Toward the Rio Grande
and I Meet Sula

The morning after the surgery, Núñez examined his patient's wound and found it healing rapidly. He instructed the man to expose the wound to the sunlight when the sun was well up and hot.

I was told in sign language that the news of the warrior's healing was passing from village to village. The warrior was a well-known man whose physical trouble had been common knowledge. In two days it was apparent that the wound would soon be completely healed. The man and his kin had tried to give Núñez everything they possessed, but as usual he took nothing.

The people of this forested region were skillful hunters and there was an abundance of game. We feasted on venison almost every meal, since the hunters brought in deer each day. We also had wild turkey a number of times. There were small nuts in the cones of the pines that Núñez called *piñones*, which were good to the taste and nutritious. With all this, together with the people's wide knowledge of the many edible plants and berries in their area, we were bountifully fed. And thank goodness for that, because after leaving the mountains we were to encounter a number of days of hardship.

At first, we came to a beautiful little river* flowing down from higher mountains. It was full of speckled fish whose skins exhibited many colors. As long as we stayed close to the river, I was able to catch several of these beautiful creatures. They were delicious when roasted and very strengthening. I could not help but wish for Akka while I was here, remembering her fondness for fish.

People came out of the mountains by the thousands, bringing their sick. It became almost impossible to get near Núñez amidst the pressing throngs. Many were sick, needing his service as a healer, but many also wanted Núñez's blessing only, because they knew he belonged to the Great Spirit. No day was too busy for him to give the people a message in sign language about his *Dios*. They were most attentive to his messages and sat quietly in great crowds about him. While he was busy in the mountains, I spent many days resting or fishing along the banks of the clear, cold stream.

From a brief contact with Núñez, I found that we would follow the river as long as we could and then turn southward toward hilly country and a great round mountain that lay to the south. I laid in a good supply of jerked venison, knowing that both food and water would be scarce. After this, we would eventually turn toward the Tiguex River, or, as most of the Spaniards later called it, the Rio Grande. This, of course, was the river on which my home village was situated, although it lay far to the north.

At last it became apparent that the Spaniards were leaving these pine-clad mountains. I traveled ahead down the river, living on fish and the edible herbs and berries that were all around. Finally Núñez and his companions overtook me. At last he was free of the multitudes, although quite a few Indians still traveled with him. Some of these were guides that would con-

* Probably the Tularosa

tinue with him until he had crossed the semidesert country that
lay ahead.

As we left the mountains for the foothills, these Indians formed
long lines with each person in line armed with a club. As rabbits
sprang up and passed along the line, clubs were thrown at them.
Many of these were served up at mealtime as roasted rabbit,
something which never particularly thrilled my palate. But it
was food, and as such was strengthening.

Finally only our guides were left. They knew where the
waterholes were and the small rancherias. At each watering-
place stood a few lodges, and always a few people were sick and
needed the help of Núñez, the wonder-working medicine man
whose fame had spread over the entire country. It seemed that
the healing process never abated. It was always attended by
amazing success and the unfailing gratitude of those who were
cured.

Our trail led across dry, sun-baked plains dotted with low
mountains. The great round mountain I had seen from the
foothills gradually took shape and size as we approached it.*
With the help of Bolo and my snares, I kept the Spaniards supplied with meat, most of it from the always plentiful rabbits.

It was good to be able again to carry on conversations with the
Spaniards. My Spanish was now fluent enough to do this quite
well. We talked as we traveled during the day and as we sat
around our campfires each night. I enjoyed the stimulation and
the good feeling that accompanied our communication.

We passed along close to the high, round mountain, and
camped one night at its base near a spring and a few lodges. I felt
awed by this great granite mountain, towering above us. I would
have enjoyed climbing it, but knew it would delay us too long.

We passed this mountain and turned westward. After a day's
walking, we came to a small rancheria close to a fine clear
waterhole. It had been made by boulders falling down the ravine
to form a dam. There were a few Indian families living nearby.
A path led down to the waterhole through great boulders.

---

* The high, round mountain was Cerro Alto in the Hueco Mountains.

An Indian man from one of the lodges became friendly toward me and invited me to sleep in his lodge and share his food, which consisted of fish caught from the deep waterhole. His name was Kamana. That night after we had eaten, he told me an interesting story. He did this with sign language very effectively.

He said, "We have climbed the high mountain many times. Once three of us went up to the very top. On the way we had to scale a high granite face. There was a crack in it which gave purchase to our hands and feet. But it was a high, hard climb.

"As we went higher up the mountain, we came to a ridge. We were very quiet as we climbed it, and when we could look over the ridge, we saw sitting only a short distance away a great golden eagle, preening his shiny copper-colored feathers.

"This was closer than I had ever been to an eagle. His curved beak was strong and cruel looking. The talons on his toes were long and equally cruel looking. I knew what this bird could do with his beak and talons. Once I had seen a golden eagle attack a young antelope. First, he descended on the half-grown animal and sank his talons into its back, crippling the hind legs. The antelope fell, and then the eagle attacked its eyes with his strong beak. He was joined by a second eagle, and together they tore at the flesh of the antelope and ate their fill.

"Knowing the power of this bird gave me a great respect for it. We watched the eagle a long time. Finally the bird seemed to sense our presence. With a powerful spring and beat of its wings, it started flying upward. Up, up, up it circled until it was only a speck in the bright blue sky."

I can see Kamana now in memory as he described the upward flight of the eagle. He rose to his fullest height, his hand circling over his head. He threw back his head as he recalled watching the big bird. I could feel Kamana's ecstacy as he told of the big eagle.

He went on with his story. "We climbed higher and higher. We came to a place where great boulders had fallen down the mountain to make a grotto." Kamana then drew me a picture on the ground. It was a view from above of three great boulders.

"A flat rock had fallen on top to make a roof over the grotto. Not far away was a tall heavy rock like a spear thrust high up toward the sky. This rock was balanced so that even a strong breeze would make it sway. A slight push of my hand could set it in motion. Yet it was very big and heavy." Then Kamana drew me a picture of the balanced rock.

He went on: "It was a holy place. From this high on the mountain we could see long, long distances away. From this height we could begin to see how big was the great world where we lived. Each of the three of us spread our arms to the sky and worshiped the Great Spirit.

"As we went down the mountain we were silent, because we had felt the presence of the Great Spirit."

I was glad to hear Kamana's experience. It helped me to know that the Great Spirit has many people of all kinds who seek Him and worship Him. Many of these are humble, poor people. As I slept that night, I felt a great reverence and sense of peace.

Two women had joined our company several days before we came to Cerro Alto. We learned that one of them was a Jumano Indian who had been visiting and trading in a village with the Plains Indians. Her sister had married one of the men of the Plains tribe. The younger of the women, whose name was Sula, had been a captive of the Plains Indians and had worked as a servant. With the help of the older woman, Magrana, Sula had succeeded in escaping.

Magrana volunteered to go on to the Jumanos and announce Núñez's arrival. She said that she and Sula would do this and then return to accompany us to the Tiguex villages of the Jumanos. Magrana had heard of Núñez long before she joined us. It was evident that she had a great feeling of reverence for him. She asked his blessing, upon which he laid his hand on her head and prayed for her. Her gratitude for this was easy to see. Immediately she and Sula departed to act as messengers for him. They were gone for several days.

While we were still waiting at the waterhole, Kamana warned us, "A big wind is coming. Very bad. Do not travel tomorrow. Stay here among the rocks where you will be protected."

As the sun rose, I could see a low cloud in the northwest. Watching it, I saw it was a wall of sand. The big wind had picked up the sand as it crossed the region of the sandhills.

When the wind struck it had greater violence than I had ever felt in a wind. It shook the lodges as if it wished to tear them apart. I was in Kamana's lodge. He had stored water in gourds and covered them to keep the water clean. He dampened a piece of cotton cloth and gave it to me to hold over my nose, since coarse sand and fine dust filled the air. Kamana's lodge was sturdily constructed and was not damaged by the fearful force of the wind.

About an hour after the wind started, Magrana and Sula returned to the rancheria. They came immediately to Kamana's lodge, since it was the largest in the village.

Magrana said, "I awakened very early and felt a storm was coming. We started walking in the dark and have been on our way four hours. The wind started about an hour ago." She showed us bloody scratches on her face where the wind had struck with coarse gravel and sand.

Sula said she had covered her head and face with the cured deerskin on which she slept. "I followed Magrana closely, peeping from under my cover," she explained.

As Magrana and Sula came into the lodge, I could not help but notice how disheveled and dirty they were. Their hair was tangled and covered with sand, and a film of dust coated their faces. Sula's long black eyelashes were gray from the dust, as were her eyebrows. Kamana's wife gave both women a dampened cotton cloth to wipe their faces clean and clear their eyes.

I felt that Magrana had an unusual sense of direction to have found the rancheria in the blinding storm. The wind blew hard all that day. It began to abate as the sun went down. Since the weather was almost cold, Kamana left a fire of coals burning in the lodge where he, his wife and two children, the two women and I all slept that night.

In the morning the wind died down. The sky was a pale blue and the air was very cool. Soon we had all eaten and were ready to start our day's journey. I thanked Kamana and his wife for their hospitality, and their brown faces creased with smiles as we told them good-bye.

We left the ravine and the rancheria. It was not long before we found ourselves struggling through the deep sand of the sandhills that stretched away to the west as far as the eyes could see. In the clear air the high mountains to the northwest showed up distinctly. These were the Organ Mountains that lay between me and my distant home on the upper Tiguex, which I longed to visit.

Walking through the sandhills was slow, hard work. Magrana, our guide, seemed confident about her direction and showing us the best trail to follow. The sandhills were piled up around shrubs. These were mostly low mesquite bushes and some creosote bushes. Magrana showed me that the trail was marked by twigs tied at the top of the shrubs. This I knew to be best because the loose sand was shifting all the time.

The sandhills were a haven for many rabbits—big jackrabbits and quick cottontails. Bolo spent all his time in pursuit of these rabbits, keeping us supplied with both varieties. The meat of the jackrabbits was usually tough and stringy, so I cooked none of these. But our Indian guides kept them and cooked them.

Our first night in the sandhills both Magrana and Sula came close to my fire, where I was roasting the meat of two rabbits Bolo had brought me.

In sign language I asked, "Are you hungry?"

Sula was quick to answer, "Yes."

Magrana smiled and nodded.

So we ate until we were satisfied. I then let the women cook two more rabbits which Bolo had brought me. This cooked meat would give us something for breakfast and something to eat at midday so that we would not have to stop and build fires to cook.

I gave the women one of my combs. For this they were grateful, immediately attempting to groom their hair, full as it was of sand and dust. However, both of them looked better after their hair was combed. Sula had Magrana tie her long, black hair with a deerhide thong. I became conscious that Sula, underneath the dirt, was a very attractive woman.

"Where do you go?" I asked her.

"To the Tiguex to my home." The thought that Sula was a Pueblo had never entered my mind, and here we had been communicating in the versatile sign language.

"Which way do you go?" asked Sula.

"First to the Tiguex, then far west to the Big Water, as I follow Núñez who is my teacher and leader."

She answered, "If you would go to the Big Water, follow the Tiguex to the Rincon Ford, then turn west and guides will show you the way."

I was of course familiar with the Tiguex, not only with the great gorge close to the Rincon Ford but much farther north.

Sula was dressed in a durable cotton blouse, now much in need of washing. She wore a knee-length skirt of deerskin. It was darkened and unclean. Her legs were sturdy but well formed and graceful. Her face was kindly and bright, with high cheekbones, a broad forehead and a mouth that smiled easily. Her mouth was beautifully shaped and her lips full and red.

When I remembered Sula had been in captivity and had escaped, and the long journey she and Magrana had taken for Núñez, I could excuse her lack of cleanliness. Also I sensed that she was a very fine person underneath the wear and tear of her escape and difficult traveling.

The next night again the women joined me as I cooked. Sula helped me and sat close to me. She was a pretty woman and I was glad she felt attracted to me.

The trek across the remaining sandhills was dry and tedious and slow. Finally we stood on the edge of the sandhills, overlooking the green valley of the Tiguex. Shrubs and trees filled the valley. Many of these were tamarisks, willows, and cottonwoods.

Far away we could see the lodges of the Jumano village. The lodges appeared mostly permanent. Later I found they were constructed of upright poles close together. Most of the roofs were a conical thick thatch, but a few were flat. Flexible willow withes woven close together between upright poles made the walls. Cracks were chinked with grass and clay.

The village was large. As we approached, we found that the people were inside their houses, their faces toward the wall and all their possessions on the floor close to the door.

Núñez called them out and spoke to them kindly. He told them in sign language that he wanted nothing they owned, but needed food and water.

Soon the people were busy roasting meat. They prepared

beans and what the Spaniards called *calavasas* (squash). They also had corn which they ground between rocks. They told us this corn came from far to the north, since it had been so dry in their country no corn would grow.

Chapter XII

I Temporarily Leave
The Child of the Sun
To Visit My People

These villages on the Rio Grande were familiar to me. When I first left my Pueblo village and came south I visited several of them in my early trading. This was before I turned eastward to the salt lakes. Now, many of the people recognized me and were friendly to me. Of course, due to my size alone I am easy to recognize and hard to forget.

Living in these villages were the Jumanos. They had well-constructed permanent houses. Rain was rarely a threat to them, since along the Rio Grande rainfall was usually very light. Even for this dry country, rain had not fallen in so long that they told Núñez they had not been able to raise a corn crop in over two years. My people had learned the skill of irrigation long ago, which helped them raise crops even in a drought. I was surprised that the Jumanos did not know about irrigation. And with the abundance of water in the Rio Grande so nearby!

I noticed a few houses made of mats. These were more capable of being transported since the mats needed only a sturdy frame

to be tied to. Evidently some of the Jumanos liked to move
frequently.

The pillage that had taken place during much of our journey
had now stopped completely. These people were generous to the
Spaniards, giving them squash and beans and even some of
their seed corn. They were eager to feed these healers of whom
they were in awe. Even in the villages beyond the first one we
visited, the people had piled all their possessions at the door of
the lodge and were found kneeling with their backs toward the
door, in complete submission to their visitors.

I explained to Núñez the route that the two women had told us
was best if we were going toward the ocean in the west. He further inquired of the Jumanos if this was the best route, and they
assured him it was. They drew maps of the trails that let us all
know clearly the best way to go to the far west.

Every day in sign language, Núñez gave a talk to the Jumanos
about religion. In his talk he said that the supreme creator, *Dios*,
had made everything including plants, animals, and man
himself. He said that this great *Dios* was good and that He had
made laws or principles that people must live by. If people lived
in harmony with *Dios*, they would get along well and be blessed.
Núñez was very good in the sign language and it seemed the
people understood well what he was telling them. Since new
people came to the Jumano village every day, Núñez repeated
his message every day.

The Jumanos told him they believed in *Dios,* whom they called
Apalito and whom they worshiped. They all seemed to respond
well to Núñez's talks on religion.

Much of the cooking of the Jumanos was accomplished in an
interesting way. Each family had a collection of hollowed-out
gourds of all sizes. They would fill these with water and then
heat rocks red-hot, pick them up with wooden tongs, and drop
the hot rocks in the water, which soon began to boil. They would
put calabash, or beans, or meat in the gourds of boiling water
and cook them well that way. Núñez and his companions enjoyed
the change of diet, and food was not so scarce that the villagers
were going hungry.

I stayed in this village only two days. News had traveled down the Rio Grande for many miles that the great healer was here, and so crowds of people horded in bringing their sick, and Núñez was kept very busy treating them. It never ceased to amaze me that these multitudes of people with ailments and complaints of every kind went away seeming to be well.

I saw that Núñez and his companions would be busy many days. The Jumano villages extended down as far as a big river which flowed in from the southwest, which the Indians called the River of Shells and which later the Spaniards called Los Conchos. No doubt, visitors would be traveling this great distance to see him. Then, too, when the Spaniards would be free to leave, their journey up the river would take many days; they had to come as far as the Rincon Ford.

I began to arrange my own plans for this span of time. It had been a long time since I had seen my father and mother and brothers and sisters. I had changed greatly. Feeling a deep sense of affection, I determined to travel fast and pay a visit to my people of the Pueblos. Too, I wanted to tell them all about Núñez and how much he had done for me.

I started up the river. Realizing that my days of trading were over, I left my sledge in the last Jumano village and, with Bolo free, started jogging up the northward trail which was just east of the Rio Grande. In this valley, the Rio Grande curved and bent worse than a long, slim, crawling snake, but the trail avoided these bends.

I became aware that I was being followed and turned to see a figure trotting along the trail, trying to catch up with me. So I waited and to my surprise discovered it was Sula. I was pleased to see that she trotted at about the same pace as I. When she came up to me, she was not even breathing hard. "This is a tough person," I thought.

"If you are going up the river, I would go with you," she said in sign language.

This pleased me because I had become fond of her. When we were a few miles from the village, the trail came close to the river. Finding a sandy beach, I said to her, "I need to bathe, and this is a good place."

She answered, "I, too, need to wash."

So I stripped off my few clothes and went into the water. Sula, without hesitation, did the same. I did not stare at her, thinking she might be embarrassed. But she was not. I saw she was a well-formed woman. And as I stepped in I felt no shame about the shortness of my bony legs. Now I was proud of them because they were sturdy and served me well.

The water was so cold that neither of us lingered in it beyond the necessity of washing well. And we both were greatly refreshed. I used my bow and drill, which I now carried in my shoulder pack, to start a fire and we warmed ourselves.

Sula began singing a song. Hearing the familiar Pueblo tongue and the sweet voice singing, I smiled. When it was over, I said to her, "How foolish I have been not to know you were a Pueblo!"

When I spoke, she threw her arms around me and kissed me. "You are one of my people. How wonderful! I am going back after these three years in captivity."

"And my people live in the Pueblo farthest south on the Great River. I am going back to visit them after many years of absence."

The day was getting late and we decided to camp at that spot. I sent Bolo out hunting, knowing after he had killed and eaten, he would bring me food.

"How good it is to be with one of my own people," Sula said. "My clothes are very dirty. If I wash them, they will take a long time to dry; but I need clean clothes."

"We are coming to the first village of the Sumas," I told her. "Maybe I can help you find clean clothes."

"That will be a kind thing." ·

I took out of my pack the string of beads made from the laurel beans. "I can trade this for a clean shirt and blouse."

She laughed happily. "What beautiful beads!" Her eyes glistened as she looked at them.

"Wear them," I said, putting them around her neck. She laughed gaily again.

"Now if I just had clean clothes I would be beautiful." She was combing out her long black hair, burned to a reddish color where it had been exposed to the sun. Her hair was now clean and glossy.

"You are beautiful without clean clothes," I told her.

"I wish to tell you all about how the Plains Indians abducted me and kept me prisoner." As we sat by the fire she told me the story of how she was surprised and captured. They had wanted her as a servant, she told me. "I was never abused or violated. But I had to work very hard." She had watched for an opportune time and was finally able to escape.

"Now I am going home," she said. "At last I am going home!"

True to his training, Bolo brought me two large rabbits. They were larger and fatter here at the river bottom. Sula and I ate until we were satisfied and cooked what was left over to save for breakfast. Bolo had always liked Sula and now he came up to her for caressing, which she enjoyed.

As bedtime approached I began to pull grass to place under my buffalo robe. Seeing what I was doing, Sula began to do the same. But I noticed she had only two thin deer hides to wrap around her as she slept. Finding two buffalo robes in my bundle, I offered her one. "Here, take one of my buffalo robes. It will keep you warm; you don't have your companion to keep you warm."

"No, she is back with her husband in the village of the Jumanos. I shall miss her. She helped me very much after I escaped. But I shall have a better bed partner." She laughed and caressed my cheek. "If I didn't like you very much, I wouldn't sleep with you. But we shall keep each other warm."

This made me feel happy. Sula found me acceptable as a friend and as a man. I had found her very desirable, but had not planned to put any pressure on her to accept me. Yet here she did it voluntarily!

So we slept together. She caressed me and I delighted in the feeling of her. We made love and both enjoyed it greatly and fell sound asleep and slept all night. We arose in the coolness of daybreak, warmed our leftover rabbit and soon were going north up the trail which led from village to village of the Sumas.

Sula was a good traveler, with a great deal of endurance. We talked easily and freely. I told her why I had left the Pueblos and became a trader. She heard the story without comment.

At the next Suma village, I told Sula, "Keep the necklace. It looks good on you. I think I can trade something else for clean clothes."

Luckily, we found a young woman, about Sula's size and build, washing clothes near the village where the trail came close to the river. In sign language, Sula explained what she needed.

I took a comb from my pack and, in sign language, told the Suma woman we would give her the comb for a clean skirt and blouse. She was pleased to get the comb. Then, hanging the clothes she was washing on a tornillo tree and taking the large piece of yucca root called *amole*, which she was using for soap, she led us to her house. Sula changed in a hurry and emerged looking clean and pretty. I felt pleased with her. She was an attractive woman. I was happy to have her as my companion.

In three days, we were at the village at the mouth of the gorge at Rincon Ford. The village was on high ground beyond the reach of floodwater with well-worn paths leading around the boulders to the river.

The people of this Suma village remembered me and offered us a small mat lodge at the edge of the village in which we could sleep. Also they shared their food with us, the flat cornmeal tortillas which were very nourishing, beans well-done and flavored with herbs and venison. Food was plentiful here and several families gave us strips of venison dried in the sun, and a supply of tortillas.

Very early the next day we started our trip through the *Jornado del Muerto* as the Spaniards later called it. It was, of course, rough, unfriendly country. Twice I opened pincushion cactus, whose pulp we ate generously because of its moisture.

When I first left the Pueblos it had been spring and cool. Once again, I was lucky to be traveling north in this stretch of forbidding country in cool weather. As we kept climbing toward the high country, we were grateful for our buffalo robes as we slept.

The next night we slept close to water, the only available spring in the entire stretch of ninety miles. Below the spring was a small, rocky pool in which we bathed, although the water was very cold. Our fire after the bath gave us welcomed warmth and cheer. As usual, Bolo had brought me two rabbits and this fresh meat made a tasty meal before we slept.

The next day I filled my water bag and gave it to Sula to carry, since I carried the buffalo robes, my bow and drill for fire making and what jerked venison we had left from what the Sumas gave us. The trail was rough, making it difficult to find paths smooth enough to trot on.

As we approached my home, in Senecu, I found that I was looking forward to seeing all my family and friends again. We entered the village before sundown and met my father before anyone else. He embraced me and I told him who Sula was and that she was going home to a Pueblo a day's journey from ours. Soon friends were crowding around us and I felt the warmth of their welcome. My mother wept and laughed as she embraced me. No longer was there any of the former shame about my size in her loving welcome of me.

Donash, the shaman, after his friendly reception, said to me, "In the Kiva tonight you must tell us the most important things you have seen and learned. I can see you are a very different person from the one who left our village years ago. I can see you have much to tell. The whole village will wish to listen to you."

That night the entire village met in the Kiva and I began to tell them of my travels. I told them of standing on the beach of the Big Water where the eye travels mile after mile toward the distant horizon and sees nothing but water. Many of them had heard of the Big Water, but few had ever known anyone who had seen it.

Then I told them of Núñez and the wonders of healing that had occurred in all the villages. Rumors of this had reached them, too, and the shaman had heard of the operation in which Núñez removed the arrowhead. There was great silence as I told them of Núñez's power and how he seemed to be used by the Great Spirit.

It was late when I finished that night. There were many questions. Before retiring to our sleeping quarters, the shaman said, "We want you to continue this tomorrow night." And my father came up to me and patted my shoulder, his eyes brimming with tears. Then my mother gave me a big hug and a kiss, and I could see she was filled with pride in me. This was food for my soul.

Without question, my family provided Sula and me with a comfortable private room. Sula said to me sleepily, "I learned so much and it was wonderful!"

The next day Sula, my father and mother, and I were eating together. Sula turned to my parents and said, "Something I want to talk about is important to me. I have not discussed this with Cazador, your son, but I would be honored if he took me as his wife. I've never known any man I liked as well or enjoyed so much."

My mother's face lit up and my father's brown face wrinkled with smiles. This was something both of them had wanted so much and which, several years before, had seemed impossible.

Then Sula continued. "Cazador has told me of his plans, and that he feels that he must continue with Núñez to the end of his journey. This I understand. I have never known a man like Núñez. I watched his healing in some of the rancherias, and in the villages of the Jumanos. I do not understand these wonders but, as Cazador told us last night, this is the work of the Great Spirit, showing us how much He cares for all of us. I only wish Núñez could come to the Pueblos. So, while I would like to marry your son immediately, I know it is not possible. I shall leave him free to continue his westward journey. If he comes back and I have not married by then, I shall be pleased to marry him at that time."

This came as a welcome surprise to me. My father was at last rewarded and my mother was made happy. I knew that Sula was a beautiful person and if I were to decide to stay in the Pueblos I would have been pleased to have her as my wife. My mother and father both agreed that if it could be worked out, they would be happy for this to take place.

When I was alone with Sula later in the day, I said to her, "This is a fine thing you have done, and I love you for it. I want you to know that if I felt I should remain with the Pueblos, I could not find a more attractive or compatible wife. In this short time, we have come to know each other well. But, as you said, I must go with Núñez, and what will happen no one knows. You must not wait for me. If you find a good man and wish to marry, do."

Sula's eyes filled with tears. "You are a good man, Cazador! An honest man and, best of all, a loving man. What you say is right, and I wish you well even if I never see you again. These tears I shed are my last. We have had such a happy time together. When I tell you good-bye, I hope there will be nothing but smiles."

That night in the Kiva was my last meeting with my people. I told them the story of Núñez's Jesu-Cristo, his death and resurrection. I told them also of the dead man in the Susolo village who had been restored to life. Once again, they listened attentively and carefully.

The village leaders and the women told me as we parted, "We understand that you must go with Núñez. But we would be honored if you would come back to live with us." With the deepest gratitude I thanked them.

That night was also my last with Sula, and our love was sweet and good. Because Bolo liked her so much, I gave him to her. I would miss him, he had been a wonderful companion to me.

Early the next morning after I ate and was about to leave, my father and the shaman came to me. "We will travel the first few miles with you," my father said.

So we started down the trail to the *Jornado del Muerto*. It was a help to have their company and well-wishes. After about five miles, I knew they had come far enough, and I paused. The shaman embraced me. "I think of you every day," he told me. "I am proud of you. Of all the people of the Pueblos you have gone farther than any." My father threw his arms around me and could not speak because of his emotion.

Then they were gone and I was traveling down the long trail— alone for the first time in many years, without even the good company of Bolo. And yet, now that Bolo belonged to Sula, I felt secure about him as his declining years set in.

Leaving Sula was hard. I realized had I met her before I first left the Pueblo, I would have welcomed marriage to her. And yet I knew that what had happened to me was best. The triumph of my return to my people, their new attitude to me, this alone was worth all my years of traveling and all that had taken place.

I faced the rough southward trail with joy. In fact, it seemed that every part of my body was alive with joy. As I passed the lava fields, even these brown tumbled rocks, that the learned had told us were once molten rock belched from the earth, seemed to have a glow of unusual light about them. Usually this chaos of boulders had seemed ugly and forbidding to me.

What made it I do not know, but the whole world about me seemed transfigured. Perhaps it had been the love and respect and honor paid me by my people; perhaps it was the affection of the shaman who was a man touched by the Spirit; perhaps it had been my father's great love which still seemed to radiate about me more brightly than the sun rising over the rugged earth. And I am sure Sula's love was partly responsible.

It seemed to me I was feeling the presence of the Spirit in myself and in everything about me. Everything seemed to be in harmony and I was in harmony with everything.

Here I journeyed where most men dreaded to go. And the desolate, wild country around me seemed bathed in a strange radiance and my body felt light, almost as if my feet had wings.

Now I understood Donash's harmony with the Great Spirit. Touches of this had come to me ever since my first meeting Núñez, but nothing like my present feeling of oneness with everything about me. I sensed a life in everything: in the sky, in the great rocks that once only seemed ugly, in the creosote bushes, in the few animals and birds that I saw, in the earth under my feet. And most of all was a feeling of complete life within myself, all my thinking, and the way I felt. I knew that Donash had known many years before that this would happen to me.

I was sure that this experience of harmony with the Great Spirit would change my life. I would never be the same again. I did not know specifically what was in store for me, but I felt that whatever it was it would be good. For the present this was enough.

I was also certain that my life as a trader was over. I was no longer interested in trading goods. My experiences in sharing my knowledge with my people had given me a taste of what I liked to do and could do.

I traversed the *Jornado del Muerto* in three days, long days that seemed short, and it was almost like a waking dream. I had left my village well supplied with jerked venison and warm clothing and two newly tanned buffalo robes, between which I stayed warm these frosty nights.

The Suma villagers at the Rincon Ford told me that Núñez and his company were two days ahead of me on the westward trail. It took me four days of lonely travel to overtake them, however, though I never seemed alone on the trail. I had a certainty that a great love was in me and all around me, and that the Spirit was my companion.

I overtook Núñez before he and his guides reached the Chiricahua Mountains. They had not eaten well since leaving the Rincon Ford.

"In one place there was nothing but *paja* (hay) to eat," Dorantes told me.

Núñez laughed, "He means herbs. They had a supply of dried herbs in that village, but no meat. We needed something besides meat."

"Paja, pura paja" (Hay, just hay), grumbled Dorantes.

Núñez looked at me carefully. "Cazador, you look different. The trip to your home did you good."

"How do I look different?"

"Una resplendor nueva en su cara!" (A new radiance in your face!)

"I left in shame. I returned to my people with faith and confidence and love. My people paid me honor. I told them of you, Núñez, and the wonderful things the Spirit is doing through you."

"I wish I could go to your people. I wish I could reach everyone in the whole world. God's goodness to me makes me grateful and humble. I am a man many times blessed, Cazador."

"And I, Núñez. You have said that you see a new radiance in my face. These few days traveling alone I have felt a new radiance in all the world about me, as if I saw the glow of the Great Spirit in everything."

Núñez laid his hand on my shoulder and looked into my eyes, "You are a man of God, Cazador."

"Well, I am glad to be back with you for many reasons. One is that you shall have more meat to eat."

"Where is Bolo? That fine dog of yours! He was almost human."

"I left him at home. He needs to be in one place as he gets old. And now that I am no longer a trader, I can do without him. He has been a fine companion!"

As we awakened in the morning, I could see the Chiricahua Mountains blue in the distance to the southeast. Now that we had left the southern edge of the Colorado Plateau behind us the weather was warmer. My unfailing snares held enough rabbits for all the Spaniards to get their fill of meat before we set out on our day's journey. Of course I had my bow and arrow with me for small game. The rabbits were tame and easy to kill, so I kept the Spaniards well supplied with food and each night set my snares.

As I had felt before, I knew that my life as a trader was over. My experience with my people in Senecu, informing them about Núñez and his teaching, had made me feel that I would like to spend much of my time telling people that which would be valuable to them. Just how this would come about I did not know.

As we moved past the Chiricahua Mountains into lower land, always going south, the weather grew more and more pleasant. Our guides told us that we were now going toward the Sonora River into the land of the Ópatas, and that food would be in plentiful supply as soon as we reached their first village. We were told that we would have ample corn, squash, beans, and plenty of meat. The people also grew cotton, from which they made clothes.

Núñez and his companions, even in the colder weather along the base of the Colorado Plateau, had continued without clothes as had been their custom since living with the coastal Indians. The only concession they had made to colder weather was to wrap cured deer hides about them for some protection. They had the comfort of buffalo robes to sleep on, and that was a boon.

Chapter XIII
The Child of the Sun Among the Ópatas

Núñez had completed twenty days of hard travel from the Rincon Ford. We found ourselves in a basin, where the land dropped to form a valley. Soon we were met by men from the first Ópata village. They guided us past many plots of ground with good soil, and these were in cultivation.

The village we came to had permanent houses of several kinds. Some were of woven mats, but others were of pole construction—some with flat roofs and others with thick, sloping thatch to shed hard rains. A few had walls and roofs chiefly made of bundles of canes with heavy thatch over the canes of the roofs.

These people seemed to live better than any we had found in our journey. The women were dressed in clean cotton blouses and knee-length deerskin skirts. They reminded me of my own people, the Pueblos.

The Ópatas had heard of Núñez's power to heal and soon were bringing their sick to him, with the same hard-to-believe results. At least, improvement *seemed* apparent in every patient.

A strange thing occurred in this Ópata village. I noticed

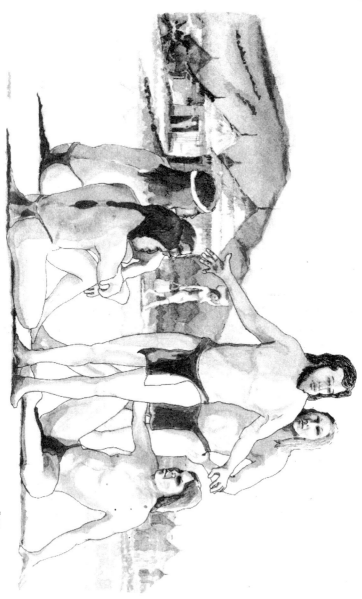

Núñez met with the Ópatas.

people were unusually friendly to me. They brought me food and showed signs of respect. Then an important man of the village came to me and in sign language invited me to his house.

He told me, "I am the shaman and I welcome you as a special guest. Our people honor the little people like you, because we feel the Spirit has sent them to us for a special purpose.

"We have a legend that when we die, our souls go to a large lake. On the north shore of this body of water lives Butza Uri, a dwarf who receives them and takes them in a large canoe to the south shore. There they find an honored old woman, Hoatzique. She swallows the souls she favors, one by one. Those she does not favor she throws into the lake. She says they are spiny and she cannot swallow them. The ones she swallows live a life of plenty and happiness in her.*

"So our name for you shall be Uri. We are blessed by your presence along with the healers. We speak the Piman language which is used by nearly all tribes as far south as Culiacán."

This way I acquired a new name, which has remained with me from that day to this. I welcomed the new name because I had become a new man. The new name seemed appropriate. The myth was important to the Ópatas. Of course, no thinking man could believe it was true. Nevertheless, I was now among people who honored dwarfs; this my respected shaman, Donash, had told me about, and had told me I would find them.

It was a welcomed change to me to be an especially honored man. I had nothing about me like Núñez to make me deserving. I was certainly no healer. I had developed this wonderful sense of the presence of the Great Spirit in me and with me and around me. I had discovered I had an ability to teach people, and for this I was grateful. But I could not compare with Núñez.

Soon after, I was to meet a man who was to become a lifelong friend. Upon leaving the house of the village shaman, I looked up to see this tall, brown person, lean and strong, standing close

* This myth is recounted in "The Ópata, an Inland Tribe of Sonora," in *The North Mexican Frontier*, Carbondale, Ill.: The Southern Illinois University Press, 1971, pp. 169 ff.

to me. He was very young, probably less than 20 years. I looked
at him and his face broke into a friendly grin. He stepped
forward, gave me his hand and said, "Uri, you and I are destined
to be friends. My name is Guatél. I heard you speaking in
Spanish and I am well-schooled in that language. I am an Ópata
by birth, but was made a captive of the Spaniards along with my
family when I was only a little boy. I was separated from them
and sent to a school where I studied Spanish under priests. They
also taught all of us boys their religion in hope that we would in
turn teach our people the Roman Catholic faith. The priests
were usually kind, good men."

I listened to this with interest. "Did you run away?" I asked.

Guatél grinned. "Yes, from the very earliest I planned to do
this, and when I became tall and strong, it was easy. The priests
were really good to us. They were good teachers. But I had many
questions about their religion from a very early age. We shall
talk about that some day when we have time."

"And after you ran away?"

"I looked in vain for my family for an entire year. My father,
I heard, had been a laborer in a silver mine, but I could never
find him. My mother and brothers and sisters, too, had all
disappeared."

"My teacher, Núñez was a slave to Indians many years ago.
This thing of slavery is bad, very bad. Each of these Spaniards
was a slave of the Indians, and a very strange thing..."

"What is so strange?"

"The dark one, the big one, was a slave of Dorantes before they
ever came to this country. He is still Dorantes' slave, but doesn't
act like one."

Guatél laughed, "That dark one is different from the others.
He is always looking for turquoise and women."

"So you have already noticed that?"

"It is something easy to notice."

I asked Guatél, "Since you were born an Ópata, you must
speak the Piman language well."

"I spoke it as a small child before we were captured. I also
learned to speak Nahua and Spanish. I learned to read both
Spanish and Nahua well. I returned to this country four years

ago, and have relearned my own language, which has not been hard."

"I understand the Piman tongue is used widely. Since it is spoken by all the people as far as Culiacán, I would like to learn it."

"I shall be glad to help you. Do you think you will be living in this country?"

"Perhaps." Then I told Guatél about Muna and that I had come looking for her.

"She is in the Cáhita area. I have met her. She is truly a fine person and comes from a good family."

"I do not know that we will be compatible, but I would like to find her."

"It is worth exploring."

"Núñez is going south searching for his own people from whom he has been separated for many years."

"He must be a very good man. He will be greatly disappointed in many of his countrymen."

"Why is that?"

"Most of them are scoundrels of the worst kind. A few are good, like Núñez. There is something bad going on now which Núñez will hear about soon enough."

"Should he know about it now?"

"There's nothing he can do until he gets further south. The Spaniards are ravaging the villages, taking prisoners and making the people slaves."

"Do you think Núñez can stop it?"

"It will be a miracle if he does, but I hope he can. From what I hear, conditions are very bad."

Guatél and I found much to talk about. He began to show me the poisons that the Ópatas used in hunting and warfare; these acted defensively against those who attacked the Ópatas. The knowledge of the poisons was very important, Guatél told me. The chief one was what the Spaniards called *la yerba pestífera*, from a small tree.

"With the poison, if you scratch yourself, in a few minutes you will be dead. Two of these poisons used in hunting just make the animal unable to move for a short while. But in that time you can slit its throat."

Guatél was not interested in marrying, as so many Indian men his age. "Some day I may marry. But now I want to be free to go where I wish."

I told him about what the shaman had said to me about dwarfs.

"Yes," commented Guatél, "all through the country where the Piman language is spoken, they honor the little people and feel they are especially sent by the Great Spirit. Muna is held in high honor in her village. Some even think she has magical powers, because she does know much about what herbs are good for sickness. Muna laughs at this idea of the magical. Yet with all the honor bestowed upon her, none of the men wish to marry her; they feel a wife should be big and strong to do all the work and that Muna is too small."

As Guatél talked about Muna, she became more real to me. Before she had seemed like a dream, but now she began to be a real person.

The Ópatas were habitually clean. They bathed and washed their clothes often. They used a soap made of the roots of the yucca, called *amole.* It lathered well and helped clean.

They gave me a private lodge and I asked Guatél to share it with me. Every day food was brought me in plenty. There was no point in setting snares for small animals anymore. However, I found that the Ópatas and the Yaquis, too, had a large net which they used to catch deer. I heard about this, but never saw it in use.

We left the first Ópata village and went down the river* from village to village. People from the nearby country brought their sick for treatment, and all talk was about the wonders Núñez performed.

Every day Núñez, when he came to a pause in his work of healing, used the sign language to teach the people about religion. And as he signed he spoke the words.

"Up above," he said in Spanish, "is a being called *Dios,* the

---

*The Sonora River

Great Spirit. He created the stars above and the moon and the sun. He created the earth and everything in it, all animals and plants, the mountains, the plains, the rivers, the seas; and He created man. From him came all good, and all good will continue to come from Him if we worship Him and keep His law. The greatest part of His law is that we love one another and treat everybody well, and that we be fair and honest. If we do these things, our lives will be good lives."

Guatél told me that the Ópatas agreed with this message, but they also had their own religion and forms of worship. Some of these I saw. The sun, to them, was the greatest of all visible things and came from the Great Spirit. They honored the sun because it made them think of the Great Spirit. Every morning, as the sun came up, the people stood to watch it. They reached their open hands to it as if to fill them with its light. Then they bathed their bodies with the light thus caught in their hands. It gave me a sense of worship as I watched them perform this beautiful ceremony. Most of them repeated this as the sun set every day.

As had happened all through Núñez's journey westward, the sick were treated. Every day I saw the sick prayed over and then leave, most of them saying they were made well. A few said they knew they would get well later because of Núñez's power to heal.

We finally came to a canyon where the Sonora River passed through the last low mountains before flowing out on the coastal plain and finally emptying in the sea. Since the water was not high, we followed the trail along the riverbed. There was another trail to take when rains filled the river to overflowing. But this trail was very rough and would take much longer. Thankfully the water was not high.

At the mouth of the canyon, built above the level of the highest floodwaters, was a large Ópata village. This was the last of their villages. While we were there, Indians came who lived by the sea. These were the Seris. They brought their sick to Núñez for treatment. The Seris were different from the Ópatas, who were usually carefree and happy, smiling, well-fed and clothed. The Seris seemed to be a sad people, underfed and completely naked except for the usual breechclout. They seemed always hungry and dejected. This, naturally, made no difference to Núñez, who treated their sick with the usual good results. He also delivered his message in the sign language about God and good relations between men.

During our stay in this village, many deer were brought in. They were of two kinds, small deer and those which were very large. Most had been shot with poisoned arrows. Guatél had shown me the small tree that this poison comes from. He had explained that if it was a time of no fruit, the juice or sap from a limb or large twig could be used successfully.

The Ópatas of this village were honored that Núñez was willing to help them. They prepared a great feast, where the only meat served was the heart of deer. Guatél told me that this feast of deer hearts was a ceremonial feast, and that the hearts of deer were the life of the deer given by the Great Spirit.

To the Ópatas, eating these deer hearts meant that the life of the Great Spirit was entering the eater and becoming a part of him. The Spaniards called this town *Corazones*, because of the feast of the deer hearts.

The rainy time of the year was upon us when we came to the Yaqui River. We found it out of its banks and impossible to cross, causing a delay of fifteen days before being able to cross on rafts made of balsa wood. Those fifteen days Guatél and I spent together. He was an artist in stalking deer and killing them with arrows tipped with poison. Together, Guatél and I kept the Spaniards supplied with venison.

But hunting took only a portion of the time. The rest of the time Guatél spent teaching me the Piman language. There were, of course, differences in the dialects from one district to another, but Guatél was well acquainted with these common differences and taught them to me. Since at that time the Piman language was not written, we used a system of writing the Piman words with Spanish letters. I used a light-colored deerhide to write the words on. One deerhide, written on both sides, held many words. I used this deerhide with my Pima words on it at night as a soft pillow.

Guatél said, "You are sleeping on the words so they will soak into your brain."

I laughed. "I sometimes dream about these Pima words."

"Would you call that having nightmares?"

And so our fifteen days waiting for the Yaqui River to subside were well spent.

Chapter XIV
The Child of the Sun
Encounters the Slave-Hunters

I knew of the activity of the slave-hunters through Guatél many days before Núñez heard of it. Guatél's reasoning was good that Núñez was very busy with his treatment of the sick in every village, and that this news of the marauding by his fellow Spaniards was going to be very disturbing to him. Consequently, the bad news might as well be postponed as long as possible.

We walked for a full day before arriving at a village where we slept. The following morning a very excited Castillo came to Núñez, bringing with him a villager who wore around his neck a metal object to which was tied a smaller piece of metal. Both were strange to me.

In connection with them, Castillo used words that were new to me. One was *hebilla* (buckle); another expression was *clavo herraduro de caballo* (horseshoe nail); still another was *cinto* (belt). Guatél, familiar with these words, explained them to me and wrote them on bark.

Núñez told me, "These are objects worn by our countrymen, and our horses have iron shoes attached to their hoofs by nails." He and Castillo questioned the man carefully.

This Pima Indian first told them the objects came from heaven, but as he went on talking, he said that men with beards had come to the river several years before. They rode on big animals, and had swords, spears and lances. They had killed two Indians, but it was not clear what had caused this.

Núñez, however, reacted to this news with, *"Que lastima que mataron los dos Indios!"* (What a pity they killed the two Indians!)

At least, now the Spaniards knew they were getting closer to their own people . . .

We traveled in mountains all the time, the trail leading from village to village, most of them along the rivers. The trail went through low mountains, most of them very rough. But to the east we could see very high mountain ranges. These were the reaches of the great Sierra Madre.

Soon we began to get news that ahead, in the land of the Cáhitas, villages were being destroyed and that Spanish soldiers were taking the Indians captive to make slaves of them.

Núñez was increasingly disturbed by this. He had been looking forward to a happy reunion with his countrymen only to discover that his countrymen were murderers.

"Núñez will put an end to this," I told Guatél.

"If he does, he is more powerful than any man I know. This mistreatment of my people has been going on for a long time. Some of the men, like my father, are taken as slaves to the mines, where they labor under such hard circumstances that they die. Some are taken to dive for pearls. These people, too, are mistreated and overworked, and are killed.

"I was an early victim of their cruelty. There may be good Spaniards besides Núñez, but I have yet to meet any except some of their better priests. Nearly all of them treat the Indians worse than animals."

The day that past winter with the Avavares, Núñez had told me of the criminal attitude of the Spaniards toward the Indians, almost in the same words as Guatél. I recalled how he confessed that his own attitude toward the Indians had been wrong and how God had humbled him as he had become a slave to the Indians. And I could see Núñez as he buried his head in his hands and wept in repentance. I remembered clearly how Núñez told me that day, "Now I am God's man at last." Now Núñez was faced with the same brutal attitude of his countrymen. What would he do? Could he do anything? I somehow felt he could, but I didn't know how. This man whom I had seen restore life to a Susolo man who was pronounced dead, who had prayed over thousands of sick people after which their health had been given back—surely a man of such power would be able to stop the ravaging of the villages and the enslavement of the Indians.

Now Guatél and I stayed closer to the Spaniards, who received more and more news about the devastation of the villages. There was also a change in their pace. They walked faster and took less interest in the ways of the people. Núñez continued to pray for the sick, but I think even the Indians sensed the great pressure upon him and that his mind was somewhere else.

Each new story of depredations of the villages made Núñez look grimmer. It was almost as if he felt personally responsible for the cruelty of his people. More news came of the Spanish soldiers burning entire villages, and taking away as many men, women, and children as they could capture. The Indians were fleeing to the mountains, we were told, where they remained in hiding in places as remote as they could find from the raids of the Spaniards. As we traveled we began to notice fields and gardens deserted. The houses were all burned.

"All of this," Guatél said, as we surveyed the ruins of a village with its deserted gardens and fields, and its houses burned to cinders, "was done by bearded people from heaven. I think most of them come from what the priests call *el infierno* (hell). I do not think they are children of the sun. They are the children of darkness and hate and lust."

"You are right, Guatél! I think Núñez is the only real child of the sun that I have ever met."

"Yes, Núñez never keeps anything for himself. He helps all people. He seems to have one idea, to help everybody find a better life. Yes, Uri, Núñez is a special person. I am grateful to you for telling me so much about him. He is a true child of heaven."

We now entered the territory of the Cáhitas. We passed through the village where Guatél had told me we would find

Muna. This was a village called Zopa. It, like so many others, had been burned and pillaged. What had happened to Muna, her family, and all the other villagers? We could only imagine the worst.

Our guides led us to a village high in the mountains in a place safe from the Spanish soldiers. Here food was abundant. There was ample corn, much of it ground into *pinole*. There was abundant venison and stores of beans. Guatél began to enquire for Muna, going from family to family. Finally he came back to me.

"I have found Muna's younger sister," he told me. "Come with me and we will talk with her."

Immediately when I saw Muna's sister I knew she was the best woman I had ever seen. She was short in stature, but not a dwarf. She was fully two spans taller than I, but when she looked at me with large, brown eyes, I knew she liked me and accepted me. I was still slow in both speaking and understanding Pima, so I let Guatél talk with her. He would then translate to me in Spanish. "She says to tell you that her older sister was a little one like you."

"Does she say her sister *was*? But what about now? Where is she now?"

Tears filled the eyes of Muna's sister, streaming down her cheeks. She brushed them away impatiently. "Muna was captured by the Spaniards and taken away in chains. Men of our village followed and shot arrows at the Spaniards from cover. But the metal suits of the Spaniards protected them. Muna died the third day after she was captured. Our men found her thrown aside and not even given burial. They brought her back to this village where we buried her. She had taken care of me since I was small. We had all left our village after she was taken captive and came up here to live with our kin high on this mountain where it is safer."

"I heard of Muna several years ago in a far country and have come all this way seeking her," I told Guatél in Spanish and he spoke rapidly in Pima to Muna's sister, whose name I found was Ara.

"Yes, she was small like you. She was a second mother to me, always watching out for me and caring for me. Everyone that

knew her loved her. I wish you could have known her. That she
was so small did not keep her from being a useful and lovable
woman. I can understand that, like her, you are not ashamed of
being so short and that your size doesn't keep you from living a
full life. Anyone can see that you are very strong and can do your
work well."

There were several children playing near us, and one of them,
a small boy, let out a cry of pain.

"Ara, Ara, he has a thorn in his foot," they called.

Ara ran to the child quickly. We went with her, thinking we
might help. But she needed no help. She examined the thorn in
the boy's foot and said to him, "Hold on tight to this tree and lift
your foot up. Squeeze the tree hard." The boy held the tree and
she caught his lifted foot. She quickly pulled the thorn out and
then told a little girl to run to one of the houses for some ointment. Then Ara held the boy close and caressed him, wiping
away his tears. "The hurt will stop soon," she said, her voice
calm and comforting. She took the ointment from the little girl
and applied it to the wound. She was tender and loving to the
hurt boy, and there was beauty in her face and the way she
moved. When she had done all she could, she joined us again.

"We are glad to have you in our village," she said to me. "I
grieve that you could not have known Muna. She was a beautiful
person. If we had come to this mountain sooner, she would not
have been captured. You are welcome to stay here. It seems safe
from those murderers that are ravaging our villages. You have
come with the good bearded stranger, the healer. We have all
heard of him and the good he does among the people. Why is it
this one is so good and the others so evil?"

So I told Guatél to tell her that Núñez was possessed of the
Great Spirit, the Giver of Life.

"And these others are possessed with the spirit of death. How
did this Núñez come to be so great and good? All of our villages
need such a man. The word of his goodness and his help to the
villages travels from town to town all over the country, until any
village where he goes will welcome him. I would like to know
how he became so good."

"It is a long, interesting story, Ara. When I come back I will tell it to you."

"Oh, you are coming back then? I would like for you to come back."

Strangely, I had not known before I said it that I was coming back. Now I could see clearly how much I wanted to come back, and because of Ara.

"Yes, I wish to come back. But I must go on with Núñez until his mission is accomplished."

"His mission?"

"Yes, he would do anything for the Indians. He is angry that his countrymen are destroying your villages and taking away people as slaves. He feels this is a great evil and will do all that he can to stop it."

"The men on animals may kill him if he tries to stop them."

"Núñez does not fear death. He does not fear anything. He is a man of great faith, great courage and great love."

"I will be waiting for your return," she said, and laid her hand on my shoulder in a friendly way.

"Núñez is ready to leave, so we must go. I hope it will not be for long."

"I will be watching for you every day," said Ara. "Come back quickly."

After we left Guatél said, "She likes you very much."

"I think that Muna's having been a dwarf helps her to understand me, and perhaps to like me, too."

"You must, of course, come back," Guatél answered.

My memory for faces is good. As I left I could see Ara's face almost as if she was there before my eyes. And I knew from that wonderful face, and the atmosphere of love and goodness that I felt coming from Ara, that she was an unusual person.

Núñez was now a man in a hurry. I was glad he was going as rapidly as possible, because I wanted to return to Ara as soon as I could.

Núñez had only one purpose, and that was to overtake the raiders. Messengers who had been sent ahead returned at noon one day saying that the next village had been completely deserted because of the nearness of the raiders.

"Look," Núñez had pointed out, "here are the stakes to which

their horses were tied. We can overtake them quickly. Castillo
and Dorantes, why don't you travel ahead as fast as possible and
we will catch up with you after you have detained these brutes."

We had been going at a hurried pace. Dorantes and Castillo
both said they were exhausted. Núñez himself had been under
great strain, but his strength seemed inexhaustible. He was a
man of great purpose.

So we rested and the next morning he and Estevánico, several
of the Pima, Guatél, and I went on in search of the horsemen.
My experience in tracking pointed the way and in about ten
leagues we overtook four mounted Spaniards who had tied their
horses and were resting by a waterhole.

As we walked toward them they stood up and looked at us in
amazement. Núñez was burned bronze by the sun. Estevánico
was dark, very dark. Each had long black hair and a bushy
beard. The two were naked, except for breechclouts.

Núñez spoke to the soldiers in Spanish which was clear to me.
"I am Álvar Núñez Cabeza de Vaca, from the long lost Narvaez
expedition to Florida in 1527. Take me to your commander."

There was something majestic in his straight, strong figure
and his resonant voice.

"But Narvaez—he and his men were all lost," said the
spokesman for the four soldiers. "This cannot be! It is a miracle!"

"Yes," answered Núñez, "it is a miracle. By the grace of God,
we are here, four of us—"

"Our commander is not far."

They led the way.

Their leader was Diego de Alcaráz, who listened to Núñez's
story. Then he sent three of his soldiers and fifty of the armed
Nahuas, who were on foot, back to get Dorantes and Castillo.

"I would like to know the exact day and month and year,"
Núñez said to Alcaráz, who told him the date. "We have come on
foot among Indians for two thousand leagues."

Alcaráz soon began telling Núñez of his own troubles. "The Indians all flee from us and we have no food."

"They flee from you because of your greed and cruelty. If you
treated them kindly, they would be kind to you."

Alcaráz muttered angry words under his breath which I could

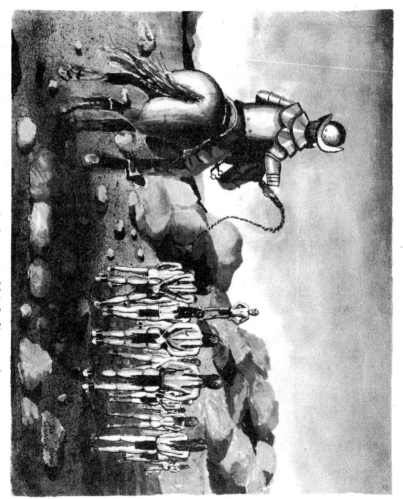

Núñez confronted Alcaráz and his Indian captives

not understand. His frown showed his extreme displeasure.

"You enslave the Indians," Núñez continued. "This is a grievous sin against God and against your fellow man. You have no right to destroy wantonly as you have been doing."

"Our governor, Guzmán, has given me permission to do this."

"Then Guzmán will be punished as you will be if you continue in your evil ways. No man has the right to such barbarity!"

There were more harsh words between the Spaniards. I felt great pride that Núñez spoke with force and clarity. He did not hesitate to condemn Alcaráz and his men.

It was five days before Dorantes and Castillo, in company of some six hundred Indians, came to us. The Indians brought food to give to Núñez, who passed it on to Alcaráz and his soldiers who were complaining of great hunger.

I saw the satisfaction and greed in Alcaráz's face as he saw the great number of Indians. I was standing close to him. "At last we shall capture a large number of slaves," I heard him say to his followers. When I safely could, I told Núñez what I had heard.

When Núñez heard this, he told Alcaráz, "You are not to touch these people. They are free people and shall remain free. Keep your hands off of them."

For the time being Alcaráz said no more of his purpose to capture the Indians as slaves.

Núñez told the Indians they should all return to their villages and begin planting and raising food. This, they said, they did not want to do, for they knew it was their duty to go with Núñez to the next Indian village.

Alcaráz had an interpreter who knew the Pima tongue as well as Spanish, and who told him of the great loyalty the Indians had for Núñez and his companions. This angered Alcaráz. Through his interpreter, he told the Indians, "These men," and he pointed at Núñez, Dorantes, and Castillo, "are murderers and are subject to us. They have no power and you must obey us rather than them."

Now the Indians began to talk among themselves. "This stranger lies," they said. "He is not the same as the Child of the Sun, who brings us life and healing; this cruel soldier brings us death and enslavement. Núñez wants nothing for himself. The soldier wants everything for himself. Núñez returns that which is given him. The soldier rides a dragon and wears metal clothes and carries a lance with which he kills. This soldier is a liar and a bad man."

This is what I heard as the Indians talked among themselves. Guatél supplemented what I did not understand. The interpreter told Alcaráz what the Indians were saying and Alcaráz was angrier than ever, cursing and raging. After much persuasion, many of the Indians consented to return to their villages.

"I will send you to Culiacán," Alcaráz told Núñez. "Cerebros, an *alcalde* who rides with us, will take you. This matter must be settled by an appointed official."

Núñez, wanting to talk with the *alcalde* at Culiacán, decided to go with Cerebros. Naturally, Guatél and I went with the other Indians who were appointed to go with them.

Cerebros must have had his orders from Alcaráz. He led us mile after mile into wild mountains. We could find no water. The Indians who were with us were poorly fed and not inured to hardship as we were. Several of them died from exhaustion and thirst. After much difficulty we came to a village from which Cerebros went on to Culiacán. Messengers left the village to carry the news of Núñez's whereabouts the eight leagues to Culiacán.

Fortunately for Núñez, Melchior Diaz in Culiacán was a man of great integrity. After listening to both Cerebros and the Indian messengers, he started for the Indian village where Núñez was resting. With him came a number of people. They were all riding good Spanish horses.

Diaz dispatched one messenger to Alcaráz with written orders for him to release any Indians held captive.

Shortly after Diaz's arrival, I saw a man who was soon to become a part of my life. He was a priest by the name of Fray José. Seeing him for the first time, I had something of the same feeling I had experienced for Núñez—a knowledge that he, too, was a child of the sun.

I was talking with Guatél in Spanish, when Fray José came up to us. His voice was deep with undertones of kindness. He said to us, "I am a teacher, and I wish only to help the Indians, just as Melchior Diaz wishes to. But I wish to live among them and teach them. I notice that both of you speak Spanish."

We told him who we were. "Yes," I added, "we speak Spanish, but only Guatél speaks the Pima language well. I am learning it and can speak some and understand some."

Guatél spoke. "He learns quickly and can already talk a great deal. Of course, later he will speak much better. He speaks Spanish much better than I."

"Where did you learn Spanish?" Fray José asked me.

"I have been traveling with Núñez a long time. He has been my teacher. I have learned to write and read many words, too."

"I want to hear all about this unusual man, Núñez. We received news of him about a month ago from Indian messengers from the north. We all know about the Narvaez expedition to Florida and how no word was received from him. That these four men have survived and have accomplished their mission is the hand of God. Now I wish to teach the Indians and learn their language. The two of you may be the ones to help me. I need much help, not only with the Pima language, but to know and understand their ways."

"Guatél is of the Ópatas who speak the Piman language and can give you much help."

"And from what people do you come?"

"I am from the people that Núñez and his companions call the Pueblos. We are people who have built villages on the high, protected places. My own village is on what we call the Tiguex River, which the Spaniards call *el Rio Grande*. Our towns are houses of many levels, one above the other."

"Oh, yes, the reports say there are great riches there."

"The reports are wrong. We are a simple people who love one another and who wish to live comfortably, with good clothing and enough to eat. We grow corn, and squash, and beans. But riches? No, not what your soldiers call riches. We do not care for gold. It is too soft a metal for usefulness. We have no sparkling gems. We have an abundance of the blue stone, turquoise. It is pretty for decoration. Tell your arrogant soldiers and rulers we have no riches of the kind they have greed for."

"Yes, I shall tell them, and try to get them to understand the truth."

"Will they believe you? We only want to be left to live our own lives."

"I hope they will believe the truth. If any of our people go to yours, I hope it will be only to teach and help them."

"My people are wise and have been since ancient days. If they can have a teacher and leader like Núñez to go to them, I would be glad. Such a teacher would be welcome."

"These are good words and I hope they will be followed."

Fray José was a man of goodwill. I knew this by the feeling of friendship he had for me. Guatél later told me that he, too, felt this great goodness coming from the person of Fray José.

Now a number of Pima Indians began to come into the village. We talked with them.

One of them said to us, "Most of the Indians who had been captured by the slave-hunters went back to their villages as Núñez had directed them."

I asked them, "Did the slave-hunters give them any more trouble?"

"Núñez had promised all the people that they would be safe. When the slave-hunters came to a village, the villagers came out bringing them food. The Spaniards were no longer cruel and greedy, but seemed docile and almost friendly. Now the slave-hunters are riding toward Culiacán."

We passed this good news on to Fray José.

"This man Núñez is a man of great power," I told him. "He works not by force but by power of the Great Spirit. This is why he does so much good. He has no weapons but only the weapon of his harmony with the Great Spirit."

"I am beginning to understand this man. He has the same intentions that I have," the priest answered.

"All our people will welcome this spirit of goodness," said Guatél. "They will quickly know what such a man is. The fame of this healer who wishes us only good has spread all over the land. He would be welcome anywhere he went. You, too, will be welcome if you have the same spirit."

"I come only in love," said Fray José simply.

I spoke up. "There is a village in the mountains where you

may wish to start. We were there a few days ago. They will receive you well."

"If the two of you will go with me, I shall go to this mountain village."

Before the day was over Alcalde Diaz ordered the great throng of Indians who had now come to the village to gather together. Some of these did not speak the Pima language. There was one Indian who was able to speak the Pima, Spanish, and the tongue of this new tribe. Melchior Diaz addressed the Indians through him.

Alcalde Diaz told all the Indians that they should return to their villages, their sowing and planting. "When any Spaniards come to you," he told them all, through the interpreter, "meet them with crosses in your hands and as long as I am in command in this country you will be treated kindly. This is the spirit of Núñez and his companions who have traveled long distances among many villages healing the sick and teaching that all men should worship the Great Spirit, whom we call *Dios.*"

A spokesman for the different tribe of Indians who listened said, "We worship this Great Spirit, whom we call *Aquar,* who made heaven and earth. We have worshiped him from ancient times."

Then Núñez spoke through the interpreter. "It is as Alcalde Diaz has said. We have come thousands of leagues from village to village, healing the sick and teaching about God. Now my work here is done, and I must go back across the great water to my own people. May *el Bendito Dios* bless you all and give you life."

Several hundred Pima Indians—men, women, and children— had been following Núñez since his appearance in their villages. Sometimes they had lagged far behind, particularly since Núñez had increased his speed to catch up with the slave-hunters. All of these Pimas now straggled into the village to which Alcalde Diaz had come. Diaz suggested to them, since there was so much fertile land in the region and so much good water, that they might be pleased to settle in this region permanently.

They followed this suggestion and gradually started building their lodges and cultivating their gardens in a village they called Bamoa.

Chapter XV

I Leave the Child of the Sun
and Go Back
to my Beautiful Ara

Alcalde Melchior Diaz liked Núñez so much that he invited him to go back to Culiacán with him. He arranged for saddle horses for all the Spaniards. These men were still dressed as most of the Indian men, that is, wearing nothing at all but the customary breechclout. It looked strange to see mounted on these sleek Spanish horses, Melchior Diaz, fully and richly clothed, with Núñez, Dorantes, and Castillo, all three of them naked.

Estevánico chose to walk with the rest of us. Fray José was also afoot. Guatél, the priest and I spent our time on the Piman language as we walked. Fray José picked up the Piman words quickly. Now I was trying to speak solely in Piman and, with Guatél's help, was doing pretty well with it.

Guatél commented as we walked, "I have become more and more interested in Núñez. I would like to know him much better. He is a man of great inner power. Otherwise he could not have stopped the marauding of the slave-hunters. He did it without arms, or any other physical force.

"He is going to need a guide to Compostela, and I think I shall offer my services. He will later need a guide to take him to Mexico City, and again I would like to do it, just to come to know him."

After we arrived at Culiacán, I went to Núñez right away to tell him that he could have Guatél as a guide all the way to Mexico City.

Núñez was quick in his response. "Tell Guatél that we shall be glad to have him as a companion and as a guide."

I returned to tell this to Guatél, who said, "Uri, I shall send messages back about our progress, for I know you will wish to hear. I shall write these on soft deerskin. First I will write a line of Spanish, and under it the Piman words spelled with Spanish letters. This will help you learn and also give the village people the message in their own language."

After we entered Culiacán, I told Fray José, "I know you will wish to be with your own people. Guatél and I will spend the night in this grove of trees behind Melchior Diaz's house and be very comfortable."

We heard later that Melchior Diaz was very firm in asking the Spaniards to wear shirts and trousers in the *alcalde's* home. As shoes were more of a problem, the Spaniards continued to wear deerskin moccasins.

I was much interested in the *alcalde's* house, which was the largest I had ever seen. It was made of stone and was only one story high. But it was a very long house, having many rooms and each room had a window.

Guatél and I were comfortable in our grove of trees. We built a small fire and roasted on it some fresh venison that an Indian who worked for the *alcalde* brought us.

After we had eaten, our fire died down and Guatél and I decided to retire early. Before we slept Guatél began to talk. "I told you," said Guatél, "that I could not agree with all the teachings of the Roman Catholic Church. Somehow I have been given powers of reasoning and clear thought, for which I am thankful. There was at least one major teaching of the church with which I could not agree."

I said, "It may be the point that I have found most difficult, too. You and I think much alike. But please tell me about it."

"You heard Melchior Diaz tell the Indians through the interpreter about his *Dios*. Melchior said if we worshiped Him and obeyed His laws, all good would come to us. He said also that those who did not would suffer eternally in *el infierno*. The part about obeying God's laws I accept. But this other is unreasonable to me.

"We did not ask to be created, so we are not responsible for being here. *Dios* created us. If we are not responsible for being here, and *Dios* is, and if He is all love and goodness but also has all wisdom and power, how could He have created some to suffer for all eternity? If He is all-wise, and all-powerful, He could have invented many methods of doing away with the unwanted evil people. He could simply have blotted them out! Why would an all-powerful God, a good God, an all-loving God, find it necessary to create an *infierno* in which His created children have to suffer for ever and ever?"

"We think alike, Guatél! I raised the same question with Núñez. As wise and good a man as Núñez is, he just told me that he lets the church decide matters like that."

"As a very young boy in the Catholic school, I began to have such questions. So, I cannot accept a religion that makes the Great Spirit evil and cruel. Like you, I believe that the teacher, Jesu-Cristo, was a great good man. I am willing to let him be my teacher and leader. And many priests in this church are good men. But I can never be so stupid as to accept a teaching like this."

So ended our talk, and with the Milky Way a bright cloud above me I drifted off to sleep. We had been asleep about two hours when we were aroused. It was Núñez, Dorantes, Castillo and Estevánico.

I looked up sleepily at Núñez. *"Qué pasa?"*

"We can't sleep on those soft beds. They are too soft! If we are to get some rest, we shall have to be on the hard ground. We picked up our buffalo robes where we had left them behind the house."

I noticed that he and the others had taken off their shirts and trousers and hung them on the bushes. The next morning they put them on again as they returned to the house.

Fray José came to me that morning. "I am eager to go to the Indian village and begin my religious teaching. I do not wish to wait until Núñez has left for Compostela. We shall leave as soon as possible. Do you think you can learn to ride, Uri? I have a gentle but small mule which is comfortable to ride."

"I can try," I said. "If I fall off, I can get back on!"

He laughed. "With that spirit, I know you will learn!"

That afternoon, we said our good-byes. Núñez was to stay in Culiacán for another two weeks. I shook hands with Castillo, Estevánico, and Dorantes; but Núñez embraced me with great affection. I shed tears as I told him good-bye.

"I shall think of you every day," I told him. "I shall remember you as a child of the sun."

"Cazador, there is something I wish to say to you in parting. I intend to come back. I have prayed that my service to the Indians shall continue. That prayer will be answered. Also, I have prayed for your life and your future. That prayer will also be answered. You have made wonderful progress. Your progress in the future will be even better.

"What I would like to do is to become governor of a colony. I wish it were Mexico. I would like to show that government can be fair and honest and just. I think I could establish a government that would be good for all the people. Here in Mexico, Spaniards and Indians could live together harmoniously, peacefully. The lives of all could be free of threat. My dream is of such a colony."

So I parted from this man who had changed my life, although a day has not passed since then that I have not felt his strong influence. Fray José and I were heading north and later Núñez and his friends were to go south.

Guatél was the last to bid farewell. I said, "Sometime in the future, I think we will be with each other again. Take care of yourself.and when you can, send us any news you may have." I was to see him again much sooner than either of us had expected. And he never had an opportunity to send us any news.

Fray José had been very thoughtful of me: not only was my

mule very small, but also the saddle was small. Melchior Diaz's Indian helper lifted me into my seat. The stirrups, shortened as much as possible, were still too long for my legs, so I rode without them. The little mule, whose name was Café, had an easy gait. I found the riding smooth.

Fray José and I began our journey together. He was an interesting companion. I asked him many questions about his homeland. And I knew that, as he told me, I was also learning about the country that Núñez came from. I was eager to know everything about Núñez's former life.

The priest wanted to know all about Núñez, so I told him the entire story as I remembered it, all the way from Narvaez's bad mistake in leaving the boats. I recounted the trouble with the Indians, the perpetual hunger, and the building of the crude boats from the skins of the horses.

Fray José was especially interested in the strange way Núñez became a healer, and also about Núñez's great change in his attitude toward the Indians. When I mentioned Las Casas and how Núñez knew him and his teachings, Fray José said, "Las Casas is a great man, a real man of God, and the grace of God has worked in the life of Núñez to make him, too, a great man."

Then I told the priest that Núñez said his enslavement to the Indians was to humble him and to help him understand that the Indians were real people created by God; and that Núñez had told me, "At last I became God's man!"

The priest's eyes filled with tears. "Yes, God works with each of us in different ways to make us truly His. Núñez is really God's man!"

When we stopped for the noon meal, Fray José took a black book out of his saddlebag.

"This, Uri, is a Spanish translation of our sacred book, which we call *La Biblia!** You will be interested in all of it. But you

---

* Spain had its vernacular translation of the Bible before 1509, according to "The Bible" in the 1940 edition of *The Encyclopedia Americana* (Volume 3, page 655), by William Benjamin Smith, late Professor Emeritus of Philosophy, Tulane University.

should start with the New Testament, which has the four
gospels describing the life on earth of Jesu-Cristo and his
teaching." Fray José opened the book to a portion entitled "San
Mateo."

Then I began to read. My little mule, Café, had so smooth a
gait that I could read without too many interruptions, unless we
came to a very rough place in the trail. I had to ask Fray José
about many words, but this only increased my knowledge of
Spanish. This was the first extensive reading I had ever done
and I found it exciting.

"This translation of *La Biblia* was made for the common
people to read. This is good vernacular Spanish that is in wide
use in Spain," Fray José informed me. "We do not yet have
available a translation made by our church, which would be
better. But this has all the important truth."

I became so interested in my reading that when we stopped to
eat, I let Fray José do all the preparing of meals.

"I suppose I shouldn't have given the book to you, if I wanted
any help," he complained.

"Oh, I will help you," I told him, apologetically.

"No, keep on reading, if you are that interested. Everybody
needs to read that book and live by it."

So, with his permission I kept on reading, frequently asking
him questions about words. I had a sense of making real
progress and it was a good feeling.

Also, as I read all about Jesu-Cristo, I began even better to
understand Núñez and his compassion toward the Indians. At
times I had felt that Núñez was drunk with his power to help
people. This same sort of intoxication had been in Jesu-Cristo,
except in him healing was not the main thing. Teaching people
how to think and how to live and how to relate with the Great
Spirit was the truly dominant factor in the life of Jesu-Cristo.
Núñez had been limited in his ability to teach the Indians
because of the language barrier. He had, of course, done
remarkably well with the universal sign language.

When I lay on my buffalo robe to go to sleep that night, I
thought of my beautiful Ara. I could see her face clearly. I could
recall every detail of it, the large beautiful eyes, her short

straight nose, her full lips and the curve of her mouth. But mainly, I remembered a feeling of great kindness and understanding which came from Ara. I had never met another woman like her. And, as I had never dreamed that such a man as Núñez could exist, neither had I ever dreamed that such a wonderful woman as Ara could be found anywhere in the world.

I could remember her long hair hanging below her shoulders. There was a sheen about it that was almost like that from obsidian, except that the top of her hair was sunburned so that it had reddish tints in it. I was sure Muna had been a fine woman, but I didn't think anyone, anywhere, could be as beautiful as Ara. I knew I wanted Ara for my companion for the rest of my life. Would she like me? Would she think me strange and ugly with my large head, broad shoulders, very short arms and pitifully short legs? Even in my drowsiness, I knew I was no longer ashamed of myself, even if my body was imperfect. This is the way I was made and I now accepted it.

We awakened to a beautifully clear morning. I watched the sun rise and thought of the Ópata people reaching out their open hands to the rising sun, seeming to catch its rays, and then bathing their bodies with light. I thought of this frequently, and always it was a beautiful memory.

That morning Fray José did not have to lift me to the saddle. I had found I could climb up a stirrup hand-over-hand, and crawl into the saddle. All that day of riding, Fray José kept me telling the story of Núñez. He was amazed at Núñez's feat of surgery in the mountains of the pine nuts. And when I told him of the obsidian knife with which the cutting had been done, Fray José was even more amazed.

Fray José was most interested in Núñez's healing among the Susolos, when everyone thought the sick man dead, burned his lodge, and how Núñez had prayed for him and the man later came to life.

"Did he really revive a dead man, Fray José?" I asked.

"I don't know. Once Jesu-Cristo raised a man from the dead."

I remembered clearly the story Núñez had told me, but I wanted to hear it again, so I encouraged Fray José to tell it to me fully.

Fray José was an easy man to talk to. I found myself growing freer with him all the time. "There is one thing that bothers me about your religion," I remarked to him.

"Please let me hear about it," and as he answered I knew he would be tolerant of anything I told him.

"My people believe in the Great Spirit. They believe He is in everything, the trees, the flowers, the rivers, the rocks and even the dirt. Your *Dios* is the same as the Great Spirit."

"Yes, we believe He made everything and is in everything, but also that He exists apart from all we see, too. I have seen the combs that you make, Uri. And as I see one of your combs, in a way you are in the comb. But you are also very much apart from it."

"I see that, Fray José, and that is not what bothers me. I have learned about *el infierno* and I cannot see how a spirit with such great power and such great love, could create men to spend eternity in such a hell. If He is all-powerful, and all-loving, and all-wise, He could find a way to dispose of bad people without making them suffer in *el infierno* forever. I cannot believe in a God who is either cruel or weak!"

"I see what troubles you," answered Fray José. "I, too, and many others have had the same thoughts. Do you know of the church's teaching about purgatory?"

"No, I have never heard of it."

"People who have done wrong are sent after death into this state in which they must learn to do right. They are not released from purgatory until they learn to live as they should. Prayer can be offered for them and masses said to expiate their sins."

"That is a far more reasonable teaching than that of *el infierno.* In purgatory there is hope and expectation of escape. In the idea of *el infierno* there is no hope at all, because it never ends. That neverending suffering would make the Great Spirit cruel indeed if He creates his children and then lets them be tortured forever."

"Yes," said Fray José, "it is a hard thing to understand. But I just accept all the teachings of the church without question and let matters rest there. What I want people to know about is the love of God as shown by His son, Jesu-Cristo."

"That is a beautiful, good thing, but the teaching of *el infierno* and the love and power of God do not go together. Even with the people we know, a person can't like you and always do you harm. If I did not accept the teaching about *el infierno*, could I still become a member of your church?"

Fray José answered with some sadness. "I am afraid you could not. You would have to accept all the teachings of the church in faith."

"That would be to surrender my right to think and reason. This is given us by God, too. So we will talk no more about it. I want to know all about Jesu-Cristo and the wonderful things he did. I am eager to read all of your sacred book."

We rode in silence for a while. Finally, Fray José said, "I would like for you to teach all the villagers Spanish so they can talk with me and I to them. I will teach you at the same time. And we shall both study the Piman language."

Soon we rode into a village where we were told that the people who had been on the ridge of the mountain had returned to their homes and fields, since all the slave-hunting had stopped. The villagers wanted to know all about Núñez, for they held him in high regard. So we directed our animals to the village of Zopa after answering their questions as best we could. Before we came to Zopa, we bathed in the cool, clear water of the river. This was most refreshing.

I was amazed at how quickly the villagers had rebuilt their lodges. Nearly all signs of the ruin and devastation that Alcaráz and his men were responsible for had been cleared up. Lodges had been rebuilt; gardens and fields had been planted and were growing.

"Núñez is responsible for this change," I told Fray José. "If it had not been for him, the village would still be deserted and in ruins."

"Yes, Núñez has great inner power. Without physical force, without arms, without political influence, he put a stop to the cruel enslavement of the Indians. It is the power of God in Núñez."

I saw Ara in front of her father's lodge and waved to her. At the very sight of her I felt a great inner joy. The shaman of the village invited us to stay in his lodge.

My speech in the Piman was good enough to be able to tell the villagers that Fray José had come to help them and teach them. I told them that he wanted to learn their language and that I also wished to learn to speak it much better.

"Fray José's language is Spanish and he thinks that many of you will wish to learn it. Both he and I will teach you Spanish. Also, he is a shaman in his own religion and thinks that you will like to know about that. It is the religion of Núñez, but very few people can work the wonders that Núñez can."

The people were pleased to hear this, and told me that they would build us two lodges and bring us food each day.

The next day was a busy one. All the villagers—which numbered about two hundred people—worked together and built us two comfortable lodges next to each other on the edge of Zopa. Each lodge had a ramada in front of it. Since the Cáhitas made most of their lodges with mats, both mine and Fray José's were of mat construction. The roof of each was of closely woven thatch shaped like a cone. This made the roof leakproof.

Enelido, Ara's father, wanted to know about Núñez. In my limited Piman, I told him as much as I could. Later, as my knowledge of the language expanded, I would tell him more.

Enelido asked Fray José and me to eat at their house that night. This we did happily. They gave us venison, squash and beans. They also served us a *pinole* sweetened with honey at the end of the meal. Atara, Enelido's wife, watched us eat hungrily and I could tell she was pleased. Enelido said to me before we left for our lodges, "Ara will give you lessons in the Piman tongue every day, if you will teach her Spanish."

This was good news. Ara must have first talked with her parents about this, which helped me know she wanted it. Enelido and Atara approved of this, which made me feel they approved of me.

I think I was smiling as I went to sleep that night on mats that Ara herself had stacked in a corner of the lodge to make me a comfortable bed. She had also left me a light cover made of cotton, saying to me as she did so, "Your buffalo robe will be too hot to sleep under. This light cover should be just right." Ara was in my mind as I went to sleep.

But that night my dreams were of Núñez. One dream was especially vivid in the morning. In it, we were in an Indian village and Núñez was healing the sick. The dream was so lifelike that when I awakened it seemed as if I had really been with Núñez.

I knew this would be a good day since I would get to be with Ara. I now hoped I could be with her every day for the rest of my life.

Ara wanted to know as much as possible about Núñez. So did her father and mother. This determined all our lessons. Then, too, Fray José and I both were Ara's students in the Piman. And when I taught her Spanish, she wanted all the lessons to be about Núñez. What developed was that I would make sentences about Núñez in Spanish. Ara would repeat these sentences to me. Then she would give these sentences to me and Fray José in the Piman language and would require us to repeat them first to her, then to her mother and father and anyone else who wanted to listen.

I wrote the Piman words on lengths of light deerskin. Before long almost all the village of Zopa was learning all about Núñez and what had happened to him, as well as the wonders he had worked on his journey all the way to the land of the Cáhitas.

So I saw Ara and her family and many of the villagers every day. Ara was now a girl of sixteen summers, graceful and well developed, although she was short. As I had clearly remembered, she had a fine friendly face, large brown eyes, light skin, almost golden in color. She was all I could ever have wanted in a woman.

And I felt that her father, Enelido, and her mother, Atara, were both friendly to me. They accepted and understood me first because of their own Muna who had been a dwarf, and then because they were good people. I had a contented feeling about this village and all the people I had met on my journey, beginning with the Ópatas in the north. They were peaceful people of goodwill, as my people of the Pueblos were.

The first thing Fray José wanted to do was build a church. He decided to build a temporary building of poles and clay *(terrado)*, and later a more permanent stone building. All the men of the village worked together on this *terrado* building. It was the largest in the village.

Fray José had with him a tool called *una hacha* (an axe), which was very handy in cutting the poles that were needed. As the men worked on the church, the women cooked and fed them. So I saw Ara many times and was able to talk with her some each time. She was an alert girl, interested in everything. She asked me many questions about Núñez and his work of healing among the Indians. She wanted to know all that happened in Núñez's contact with Alcaráz and how this cruel man had been persuaded to leave the Indians alone. The other villagers were very much interested in this, too. Núñez's victory had been the beginning of a new day of freedom and safety for all the Indians of the country.

I explained to Ara the wonders of writing and showed her on bark with a piece of ochre.

"It is magic!" she said, her large brown eyes shining with pleasure.

"That is exactly what I said when Núñez first showed it to me, but look, you are making the mark wrong," I told her, and took her hand to guide it right. This was the first time I had ever touched her and it was the most wonderful feeling I ever had! Nothing had ever felt as good to my touch as her smooth, soft hand. When we were finished writing, she reached for my hand and held it again. I knew that Ara not only was a beautiful girl, but had a beautiful spirit. I would willingly have been her slave from that time on.

I was rapidly reading all of that part of Fray José's *Biblia* called *El Nuevo Testamento.* I was constantly asking him the meaning of words.

"This is written in our vernacular as I told you. It is a good way to learn Spanish and religion at the same time," he said to me.

I had finished the book of San Mateo, and was starting on San Marcos. I had a feeling of progress.

As I found verses that were good, I wrote them down and

memorized them. Then I taught them to Ara. One that she liked especially was "Blessed are the peacemakers, for they shall be called the children of God."

"Núñez is a peacemaker," she said.

When Ara learned a verse, she taught it to her mother and father. One day she asked me, "Will you accept this new religion?"

So I had to tell her, "Fray José says if I do not accept all that they teach, I can't receive their baptism."

"You do not accept all they teach?"

"No, my people believe the Great Spirit is in everything and made everything. I cannot believe this good spirit would create men to be punished eternally in *el infierno*. That is what the church teaches will happen to a great many people."

"Nor could I believe that either."

"Yet I am interested in Jesu-Cristo and the wonderful things he did. He went among the people healing, and that is just what I have seen in Núñez. Also I am interested in the sacred book where all these wonderful verses are, and wonderful truths."

The understanding between us grew. We were interested in many of the same things. Ara was interested in birds and animals and plants. But most of all she was interested in people. Without anyone asking her, she gathered the children together and started teaching them what she had learned of Spanish. She, as I, had memorized many of the beautiful verses from the sacred book and she began teaching these to the children. Many of the children soon began writing. Fray José gave Ara as much direction as he could, and sometimes I helped her with her classes.

Fray José had put up a large cross before his church building. Inside he had a smaller cross. All the village learned what the cross meant and they learned about the life of Jesu-Cristo.

Fray José had services in the church, but they were in Latin, which I was only beginning to learn, so I still could not understand them. As he came to the knowledge of the Piman language, he began to give short religious lessons in Piman, which I liked and understood. My own understanding of Piman had grown rapidly, since I talked with the villagers in it all the time. Fray José also made progress in it although not as quickly.

With our daily contact, the friendship and affection between Ara and me grew. We were both interested in religion, and so we talked often about Núñez and his teaching about his *Dios* and the great prophet and teacher, Jesu-Cristo.

Chapter XVI

The Child of the Sun Fails
in his Confrontation
with More Slave-Hunters

I was greatly surprised one day when Guatél appeared as I sat reading Spanish under the shade of the ramada in front of my lodge.

"Uri, I am back. I could not go on."

I looked at his black eyes and they were moist with tears. "I am glad to see you, Guatél. And I know your reasons for being here are good; if you don't want to tell me, you don't have to."

"I *do* want to tell you. I must tell you, because I am full of sadness. You know how great was my interest in Núñez, and he was very friendly to me. We stayed in Culiacán for fifteen days after you left.

"Núñez talked with me a great deal. I began to understand his thinking and his feeling. The aims for his life were for the good of all people, but especially for the Indians of Mexico. Although I had thought well of him before, I began to have a strong attachment to him, stronger than I had ever felt.

"Melchior Diaz sent twenty of his soldiers on horses to go with us to Compostela and we began our journey. The Spaniards took off their shoes and their clothes and started walking on this trail, as they had on their long journey westward."

"Why were the soldiers necessary?"

"Diaz said that the country all the way to Compostela had been ravaged by slave-traders. There were bands of Indians in hiding all along the way. They were all hostile to the Spaniards and would attack any Spaniard that happened by. To them, all Spaniards were enemies.

"So we left with an armed escort. For several days all went well. I had many good conversations with Núñez. In these talks it was clear that he wanted for the Indians only their freedom and the right to live their own lives. And he wanted more than that—he wanted them to know the Great Spirit as a friend.

"But on the fourth day out we overtook a party of six Spaniards, all slave-hunters, and they held captive in chains a large group of Indians. There were five or six hundred of these captives and they were nearly all in pitiful condition. Food was scarce, and the Indians were just skin and bones. With the fields and gardens deserted due to slave-hunters, and the people hiding in the forests and in the mountains or wherever they felt safe, it is no wonder they had little to eat."

"Our Cáhita country was the same way, you will remember, Guatél, when we passed this way with Núñez for the first time. But now we are free and safe because of Núñez."

"Yes," Guatél went on. "I was astonished when he opposed Alcaráz and I was even more surprised when finally Núñez won, and Alcaráz had to give up his captives. Remembering this, I had hope that these slaves on the way to Compostela, too, could be freed. And Núñez did everything possible to accomplish this.

"Enough food was carried by our armed escort so that we ourselves were well fed. But when Núñez wanted to share it with the half-starved slaves, the captain commanding the escort refused, saying that if we did, we would not have enough food for the rest of our trip to Compostela. Núñez defied him and gave all his own food to several of the captives. This angered the captain, who told Núñez if he gave away any more food, they would refuse to give him any more at all for his personal use on the rest of the trip.

"Next Núñez confronted the leader of the slave-hunters. He told him about the orders Melchior Diaz had given Alcaráz. The slave-hunter laughed at Núñez, saying that Melchior Diaz was a long way off and that he, the slave-hunter, had a permit from Guzmán to take Indians as slaves. Núñez was infuriated, but the slave-hunter paid no attention to him.

"Next Núñez asked the captain of the escort to command the slave-hunters to free the slaves. The captain refused, saying he had no authority to do this.

"I began to see that even Núñez could run up against people who refused to cooperate with him. I was, of course, disappointed. Perhaps I was expecting too much of Núñez. I should never have expected him to be omnipotent.

"We were in company of the captives two days. Every day, the slave-hunters used the whip on the Indians, lashing them without mercy if they lagged. One woman was sick and they used the whip on her, anyway. She died shortly after she was severely scourged. They kicked her to one side of the road and were going to leave her without burial. Núñez prayed over her and made the sign of the cross. She showed no sign of life at all. Finally, Núñez and his friends dug a shallow grave for her, over which they erected a rough cross.

"Once the slave-hunters were using the whip on a starving man because he would not move faster. Núñez could stand it no longer. He went to the poor captive and put his arms around him, braving the lash. The soldier kept on cruelly using it on Núñez until his back was bleeding and raw. Finally the captain interfered and stopped the whipping.

"When I went to Núñez to wipe the blood from his wounds and cleanse them, he said, 'They did worse than this to Jesu-Cristo. They not only lashed him but nailed him to a cross and killed him. I have prayed for these captives and know that God is going to set them free.'

"I know Núñez would have died for these people if he could have set them free. He is the greatest man I have ever known.

"The captain was impatient at the delay. When the burial was over, he insisted that they leave the slave party and hurry on.

"Again Núñez pleaded with the captain to free the captives before he went on. The captain replied that he had no right to deprive the slave-hunters of their property. The suffering of the captives is impossible to describe. Their legs were bleeding from the chains. They were whipped continually. All of it brought back to me the experience of my family . . . It was the same kind of suffering of both the spirit and the body. I was only a small boy at the time of our capture. After several days of beatings and starvation, we passed a chapel. The priest came out to try to alleviate our suffering. It was he who rescued me from the slave-hunters and later placed me in the mission school in Mexico City.

"The awful memories of what had happened to my family flooded back on me like a black tide in which I was drowning. Since Núñez had been impotent to free the Indians, I could no longer tolerate the sight of the captives. I had seen both my father and my mother whipped unmercifully and abused and taken away in chains. I never saw them again, although, as I told you, I spent a year looking for them after I ran away from school.

"The condition of the prisoners was unbearable to me. My disappointment in Núñez's failure to free the captives gave me a feeling of complete hopelessness. I expected some sort of miracle which he could not perform. That I overheard him say he would spend the rest of his life fighting this evil did not help. I did the cowardly thing. I ran away from something horrible and ugly that I felt I could endure no longer.

"Yet I still can't get away from the ghastly sights of the suffering of those people. I kept seeing them as I traveled this way. I had nightmares about them at night."

A shudder ran through his body. He put his face in his hands and sobbed.

"I am a coward to have run away. I should have stayed and tried in some way to free those people."

There was nothing I could do or say that would help him. I slept poorly that night and awakened before dawn. Guatél was already up, cooking meat on the open fire.

The night had changed him. He seemed to have hardened. He

said to me, "Uri, I have decided I will get a horse in Culiacán and overtake the slave-hunters. I shall kill every Spaniard in charge, even if I have to cut their throats at night."

I said only, "Guatél, I wish you well in whatever you decide to do. I know you will do anything you can to stop this barbarity."

I had my little saddle mule, Café. This animal I gave to Guatél. I said to him, "I know that the Great Spirit will help you to do anything that is necessary for the good of the captives."

Much later I was to hear the whole story. The procession of weakened captives had moved slowly, and Guatél overtook them when they were still many miles from Compostela. We heard that the captives had been freed, but we did not know how, until a long time afterward. Ara said, "The Great Spirit moves in many ways to help His children."

Like Guatél, I was disappointed that Núñez had failed to free the captives, yet the overall effect he had on the treatment of the Indians was good. Then, by government decree, the widespread imprisonment of the Indians was stopped. A movement was even begun by the Franciscans to educate the Indians and give them practical knowledge for better living.

Chapter XVII
A *Tigre* and Two Guacamayas

One of Ara's friends, an older woman, kept a green parrot with a red head in a large cage woven of willow withes. One day as I passed along, Ara was standing alone, looking at the parrot. I stopped and spoke to her.

"It's a beautiful bird and very tame," she said. "And it can say a few words. When they let it out, it will not fly away but lands on their shoulders."

I could see how much Ara liked the pet parrot.

"There are many kinds of parrots. The little parakeets are pretty," I said.

"The prettiest and smartest of all are the brilliant guacamayas.* I wish I had one for a pet."

So I began to lay plans to try to trap a guacamaya for her. Secretly, I first started building a cage. I worked on it when I could. It was to be even larger than the cage of the green parrot. Day after day I added to it, working in a grove away from the village. I wanted the guacamaya to be a surprise to her. When I finished the cage and was satisfied with it, I began to go

* The macaws

through the woods along the river, to see if I could find any guacamayas. They were much scarcer than I had thought.

But I began to construct my trap, anyway. The top of the trap was like a pyramid, and heavy enough to hold a big bird in it without it getting out. The trigger of the trap was carefully constructed with a long arm that the bird would brush against to throw the trigger. The top would then fall and the bird would be caught. There would be grain or fruit as bait close to the trigger and also leading into the trap.

I found a flock of green parrots and set my trap with corn leading to it. When I returned I had two green parrots, so I knew the trap worked well. I left the green parrots in the big cage in the grove with water and corn. Later I could use them to trade for anything I might find useful.

Melchior Diaz had promised that he would send us news of Núñez as it came to him at Culiacán. There was always passage between the villages, and travelers carried any news there might be.

The first message we had was that Núñez and his companions had reached Compostela. Since many of the Indians of this region had been antagonized by Spanish slave-hunters, they were hostile to all Spaniards. It was for this reason that Núñez had been given his armed escort of twenty soldiers. From there they were going to Mexico City.

I welcomed any news of Núñez that came my way. What I did not understand was the overpowering interest of all the Indians in Núñez. They were hungry for any small news of him and this was passed around the village until everyone knew everything that was happening to him. Also messengers came from other villages to find out about him and assured us that they would pass the news along to still other villages. The effect of Núñez's life on all the Indians was far greater than I had understood.

Most of my hunting of the guacamaya had been upstream from the village. I changed my tactics now, going downstream to lower and hotter country. I searched close to the river and ranged farther away into more remote wooded areas of the lower country.

One day I came out of the forest to see a high hill. The face of it was a rocky cliff. As I stood there looking upward, I heard the coughing grunt of a *tigre.* * I had my bow and arrows, but they would have been pitifully feeble against the powerful charge of a *tigre.* I made up my mind that in the future I would come prepared, but this helped me not at all in the situation I found myself.

I was hidden in a thick clump of trees as I heard the cat approaching. Fortunately, the wind was blowing from the animal toward me. Then I saw the *tigre* as he emerged into a clear space of bright sunlight. I could see the rippling of his muscles under his dappled coat and, even though I was frightened, the beauty of this animal was startling. He stood stock-still, looking around majestically, and all his bearing showed that he feared nothing. Then he moved away, and the rhythm of his movement was a picture of grace that I can see clearly in my memory.

However, I was relieved. I knew I had been in great danger. When I felt it was safe, I moved away from the area as fast as I could.

Still I had seen no guacamayas. In the village below ours, lived an old man that everyone said knew almost everything there was to know about all the animals, birds, and plants of this country. His name was Antaba. I made up my mind to pay him a visit. Because of my studies, however, I was delayed in doing so.

My teaching Spanish and my lessons in the Piman language took most of my time. I looked forward to these, not only because I was learning, but because I was close to Ara. When I was near her, I always felt good.

Not only was I learning Spanish, but I was learning many good things because I was reading from Fray José's *Nuevo Testamento.* I remember when Ara learned the verse *"Dios es amor"* (God is love). She first learned to say it and then wrote the letters and the words. She liked it so much that she took a piece of smooth red ochre and wrote it in large, even letters on a large piece of bark.

"I am going to hang this verse where I can see it every day

* A jaguar

when I wake up," she told me. Later she said, "This is my
favorite verse. I say it every morning when I open my eyes."

I knew my love for Ara was growing stronger every day and
hoped that she was beginning to feel love toward me. My love for
Ara was not only the love of a man for a woman, but it was the
love of something beautiful and good in Ara. I had a feeling that
the Great Spirit was in my friendship for this wonderful girl.

I finally found a day when I could visit the lower village where
Antaba lived. He was a very old man with a wrinkled face, very
dark brown. His hair was very white. There was a live gleam in
his dark eyes and I could feel his friendliness as I talked with
him.

"I have been trying to find the guacamayas, but have failed.
I thought maybe, with your knowledge of birds, you might tell
me where they are."

"They are beautiful birds," he answered at last. "The
guacamaya has the most brilliant colors of any of our birds. It
also has a very hard, strong bill. It can destroy most wood. If you
build a cage, it must be of very hard wood." This made me
wonder if my cage was strong enough.

"They are very fond of wild figs. If you know where a large
grove is, when the figs are ripe, you might find a flock."

"Do you know where such groves are?"

"Yes, I know where several groves are. Let me draw you a map.
But first I want to make a trade with you. I shall draw you a map
showing the location of several groves of wild figs, but I want you
to do something for me and the entire village."

"If I can, Antaba, I shall do it."

"You know all about the Child of the Sun. He is the one we are
interested in. The whole village wants to know about him. If you
will tell our village about him, his healing and teaching, I shall
draw you the map."

Of course, I agreed. So the whole village assembled around
Antaba's mat-house and in my imperfect Piman, aided with the
universal sign language, I spent the entire afternoon telling
them about Núñez and his great journey—his healing, and his
teaching. So that day I did not get to hunt my guacamayas. But
after several hours of talking about Núñez, as I left to return to

Zopa I felt almost as if he were walking with me. Again I was made to know Núñez's powerful effect upon the lives of the Mexican Indians.

I returned early the next day. Antaba thanked me again and again for telling him about Núñez. Then he drew me a map in the dirt before his house, showing me the locations of several groves of wild figs.

When I left him, I decided to pay a visit to the rocky ground where I had seen the *tigre*. I had brought with me several poisoned arrows. Finding a cave in the low cliff, I felt sure the *tigre* lived there. So I climbed high on the cliff over the cave. I sat on a large rock, very quietly.

My mistake, and it could have been fatal, was my certainty that the *tigre* was in his den and would soon come out. I also felt false security in my elevated position.

I began to feel uneasy. Everything seemed too quiet. No birds were singing and this seemed strange to me. I held my bow ready, with the arrows lightly strung. When the *tigre* came out, it would not require a long shot, and I would have the advantage of shooting from above.

My feeling of insecurity grew. All my senses seemed sharpened, and perhaps this was what saved me, since I seemed to hear the faintest sound from behind. I turned slowly to look back, and saw the *tigre*. He had stalked me from the rear, almost noiselessly.

I was aware of the power of his body. The sun shone on the dark spots, and reddish yellow between them. If it had not been for the great danger, I might have admired the beauty of its sleek skin and the rippling of great muscles underneath. The *tigre* was not quite within leaping distance. I saw his eyes, and sensed he was about to charge. I quickly prepared to shoot. Just as I did, the *tigre* charged and I let fly a poisoned arrow which pierced him in the chest. He was about to spring when the poison took effect. He half-leaped into the air and fell over heavily, his huge paws outstretched as if, even in death, he wished to reach me.

My mind went out in a prayer of thanksgiving to the Great Spirit, whom I felt was protecting me. I did not move immediately to the dead animal, but watched him to make sure he was dead. I was also afraid that this might be one of a pair of *tigres* living in the den.

Finally, I hauled the dead body to where I could watch both it and the den, and frequently glanced all around to make sure I would not be surprised again. Also I was supremely grateful for the quick effectiveness of the Ópata poison on my arrow. Without that I would not have had a chance to survive.

I skinned the *tigre* carefully with a sharp knife that Fray José had given me. Then I left the area of the den as quickly as I could, carrying the heavy pelt, which slowed me down considerably.

It was after dark when I threw the skin down on the ground in front of Enelido's door. News of the kill passed quickly around the village and the people all crowded around to see it.

I could see admiration in Enelido's gaze as he rubbed the spotted pelt. Then I told him, "It is yours. I want you to have it."

Enelido was pleased beyond what I had expected. He ran over to me and embraced me, giving me what Fray José called *el abrazo doble* (the double embrace).

It was the next day that Enelido and Atara called me into their lodge. "We have been thinking about this for a long time," Atara said, smiling at me. I thought how much her kind, motherly face showed her affection.

"Ever since Muna's death we have felt an empty place in our family, especially when we eat together," explained Atara. "We would like for you to take Muna's place, and for you to know that we want you to share our food with us each day."

I was so moved that my eyes filled with tears, and at first I could say nothing. At last I could talk. "It is a great honor—a wonderful, friendly thing for you to do." And as I said that, Atara came to me and threw her arms around me.

Enelido said, "When Núñez came to us on the mountain, we felt that he wanted only the best for all of us, and that he would help us in any way he could. We feel the same about you."

Of course, what he said was true. I wanted to serve the village in any way I could. This was the spirit of Núñez and, long before him, the spirit of Jesu-Cristo. I knew now what my place would be—I would become a friend to all the people with whom I lived.

And one of the ways I could be a friend to them was to teach them the way of life that Núñez practiced, which was the way of Jesu-Cristo.

I was now reading more and more rapidly. Every day I asked Fray José questions, which he always tried to answer honestly. The more I saw of this priest, the more I knew he was like Núñez in wanting only to serve the people.

Fray José was not a healer. He would pray for the sick and make the sign of the cross. But somehow the wonderful things that had happened for Núñez never happened for Fray José. Yet I knew he was a good man who, like Núñez, wanted to help anybody and everybody as much as he could.

The next news we received from Núñez was that, after staying two weeks in Compostela, he had completed his journey to Mexico City. All along the way, people had greeted him and befriended him. Melchior Diaz sent word that Núñez, Castillo, and Dorantes, were planning to stay in Mexico City for several months while writing a joint report of their long journey.

Fray José wrote a note of thanks to Melchior Diaz. He used a piece of cured deerskin and wrote with ochre. It was the first time I had ever seen a letter written.

"Es una mensaje de gratitud (It is a message of gratitude),"* Fray José said and, seeing my interest, he let me read all of it. I knew this letter-writing was a custom, and Fray José had told me that sometimes very long letters were written.

I asked him, "Is this joint report that is being written a letter?"

"It is like a letter to the king, Charles the Fifth. But it is an official report, a long document, telling of what happened to the Narvaez expedition and its survivors."

All this seemed wonderful to me, as was all the knowledge I was learning, and the skills. A new world was opening up to me because of Núñez, and I would always be grateful.

Later, carrying my bird trap, I located the groves of wild figs. The first one contained no guacamayas. The second one, however, was another story. I could hear their raucous voices before I ever got there and stood in awe of their brilliant plumage as they fed on the figs. I watched them from behind cover. No wonder Ara wanted one!

Then I saw something that made me know I would not need my trap. There were nests in a nearby grove of tall trees. Parent birds were carrying food to their young. I climbed a tree next to one of the nests and looked down on it. The young already had feathers. I now knew what I could do: I would return the next day with a bag and would capture two young birds. I had heard that these birds, captured young, tamed easily, so I knew this would be best!

The next day I returned and climbed the trees where I had seen the feathered young, and captured two young guacamayas. The parents of the young birds made loud noises and flew close to me, but never attacked me. I took my two birds back to the village and put them in the big cage in the grove. Since it was not safe to leave them overnight, I appealed to Fray José for help. In the dark, the two of us carried the cage with the two young birds back to his lodge undetected.

The next morning when I went to Enelido's lodge, I was so filled with pleasure at my gift for Ara that I couldn't hide it.

"You seem unusually happy," said Atara.

"I feel fine," I said.

"Tell us why," said Ara.

"I have a gift for you."

"What kind of gift?" She was excited by my news.

"I want all of you to come with me when we have finished eating."

So when we had finished, Enelido, Atara, Ara, her younger sister Nitól, her small brother Matél, and I all went to the edge of the village to Fray José's lodge. When Ara saw the young guacamayas in their cage, she let out a cry of joy and ran to examine them closely. Then she ran back to me and threw her arms around me. Such wonderful joy!

We carried the cage to their lodge and Ara began finding out everything she could about taking care of these gaudy young birds. She found fruit for them to eat and a small, decorated pottery bowl for them to drink out of.

"And they can learn to talk," she told me triumphantly.

"What are you going to teach them?"

"Certainly not bad words as some people do. I think I will teach them my favorite verse, *'Dios es amor.'*"

So, several times a day she would repeat this verse to them. If they made any noise at all in response, she rewarded them with fruit. Soon the birds were responding almost every time Ara talked to them. If it sounded the slightest bit as if they were talking, she gave them an extra reward of fruit. If they did not respond, she gave them no fruit at all.

They soon became quite tame and, in spite of the potential danger of their strong beaks, Ara would put her arm in the cage. Nearly always one of the birds would light on it. Then one time Ara opened the cage door wide and brought one of the birds out on her arm, gently closing the cage door. This was the smaller of the two birds, whom Ara had named Tulo; the large one was named Anak. She then put the smaller bird on her shoulder and walked about with it perched there. It was not long until she had both birds out, riding on her shoulders.

The guacamayas matured rapidly, with their tail feathers and wing feathers lengthening. Their heads and upper bodies were a brilliant red, shading to orange and yellow, with the ends of the wings violet and blue. Their long tails were red with blue edges on some of the feathers. I had never seen such colorful birds. And they were very tame and loved to be in Ara's company. Frequently now they flew along wherever she went, always returning with her. But their beaks were strong and I had to build another cage of the hardest wood I could find.

One day Ara came running to me excitedly. "I think Tulo said something. I hope he repeats it for you."

Ara stood by the cage and said, *"Dios es amor."*

Tulo made a noise. Perhaps he was trying to say it. It did not sound very intelligible to me, but it pleased Ara.

"That's a smart bird. I'll give you a good reward." Ara reached her hand in the cage with a fig for Tulo.

After several weeks Tulo could say, *"Es amor. Es amor."* Ara was as pleased as if he had learned to read and write.

One afternoon shortly after this, I went to the river, thinking I might catch some fish. And in an open place in the bright sunshine I found Ara washing several cotton blouses, using the roots of the *amole* as a very effective soap. Ara smiled and welcomed me, and I forgot my fishing and sat close to the large, flat rock she was using to rub the cotton clothes on.

"I was pleased when you became a member of our family. My older sister Muna, who was small like you are, was like a second mother to me. Since she was killed, I have missed her very much. There has seemed to be an empty place in my life and now you are filling that empty place."

"It was good of your father and mother to ask me, and I feel one of you. You are really my family and I know I am loved and wanted. But Ara, my feelings for you go far beyond this. I love you more than I ever thought I could love anyone in the world. I want you to be my wife."

Ara waited before answering. Finally she said, "My feeling for you is very good. You do me a great honor to ask me. My own feeling is to say that I will. But first, as you know, I must talk it over with my mother and father, for that is our custom from old times."

"Yes, I understand that and want you to talk with them. After you have done so, if you wish, I can go and talk with them, too."

I felt all of this was happening as it should, and that the outcome would be good.

My progress in the Piman language had been rapid. Now all my conversation in the village was in the Piman, except with Fray José, with whom I always spoke Spanish. Ara met me every day to give me a lesson in Piman. I also had several deerhides covered with Pima words and sentences written with ochre. Frequently, I reviewed these to make sure I remembered them. All my lessons were centered around Núñez—his healing and his teaching. Ara was coming to be as familiar with him as I was.

The day following my meeting with Ara at the river, we met as usual for our lesson. Before we started studying Ara said, "I talked with my father and mother. They were pleased that you want me as your wife. They told me that they wish to speak with you about it."

Following our lesson, I went home with Ara. Both Enelido and Atara were sitting in front of their lodge. They gave me a friendly welcome and Ara left us, walking with a guacamaya on each shoulder. I watched her slim, graceful figure as she walked away and knew that in her I had found the person with whom I wanted to spend the rest of my life. She was a beautiful girl with a spirit more beautiful than her face and figure.

"Ara has spoken with us," Enelido said, "We will welcome you as a husband of our daughter. If you wish, we shall have the ceremonies of our tribe after the passage of a week. My friends and I will build a lodge for you in that time."

"I would like to have it on the edge of the village not far from Fray José, since I must be with him often."

Enelido nodded. "This will be suitable."

I then said, "I have just one request to make about the lodge. I had never seen any of the Spaniards' houses until I went to Culiacán. There I saw that they had not only doors, but openings in the walls they called *ventanas* (windows). I would like *una ventana* on each side of my house. I shall have deerskins on rollers so I can close the windows when I wish, especially at night to keep the insects out. But I like the light and air that the openings in the walls let in."

"This, too, we will be glad to do."

So began the building of our lodge, a short stone's throw away from where Fray José lived. Every day I watched as the men of the village worked. They built us a large lodge with two rooms. The walls were of straight, upright poles, with woven mats on the outside. The roof was conical and thickly thatched. This made the top waterproof so it would not leak at all.

Fray José had removed his cassock and put on a cotton shirt and cotton trousers, and worked as hard as any of the villagers. He stopped long enough to give me a lesson in Spanish each day. By now I had read the entire *Nuevo Testamento* in Spanish. While I still did not agree with all the religion of the Christians, I knew one thing: I felt a great affection and loyalty for Jesu-Cristo as I read about him. When I told Fray José of my feeling, he said, "It is this affection and loyalty for Jesu-Cristo that is the important thing."

"I have seen his way of life in Núñez," I told him. "I know a man can be a servant of all men as Jesu-Cristo is followed. His way is my way."

After a week, our house was finished. The following day was the appointed date for the wedding ceremonies, which lasted most of the day. By dark the ceremony was over and the villagers brought great quantities of food for the wedding feast. Following the feast, there were tribal dances that lasted beyond the middle of the night.

After midnight, the villagers went to their houses and Ara and I entered our home happily, hand in hand. We had been given many mats and these, covered with a buffalo robe, made our bed.

As we lay side by side, I said, "Ara, this is the greatest day of my life. I followed Núñez all this way, first to learn of the Great Spirit and Jesu-Cristo. But I believe I was led this way also because of you. I feel we were made for each other and my love for you is greater than I ever knew I could have."

"My love for you is just as great and I, too, feel you came this way that I might have you as a companion all my life."

That night was the beginning of a life better than I ever knew I could have. I told Fray José of my joy and he said to me, "Jesu-Cristo said, 'I am come that ye might have life and might have it more abundantly.' He is giving you the abundant life."

Many of the villagers accepted Fray José's religion and were baptized. Fray José never brought pressure to bear on the nearly half of the village that did not. "My work is made much easier because of Núñez," he told me. "His life and service is worth more than ten thousand sermons. All the Indians everywhere, even in remote places, know about him and want to know more. Núñez's influence upon all the Indians is the greatest thing that ever happened to them. Most of them want to know more about Jesu-Cristo, who is Núñez's leader and teacher. The news of Núñez's teaching and healing has spread everywhere. Even though Núñez has left us in body, the effect of his compassion, his service and his teaching is with us all the time. It may be that his presence with us is more powerful than if he were here physically."

Ara and I, Enelido and Atara, and their younger children went to Mass each Sunday morning. Fray José told me what the Latin prayers meant in Spanish, so I began to learn Latin also.

Fray José kept close track of the months and the days. He told me that it was the month of *Abril*, the 20th day, when Núñez sailed toward his home. The message had come, as usual, from Melchior Diaz.

In talking with Ara, I said to her, "You know, I have the strangest feeling. I know Núñez is gone, that he is even now sailing across the ocean or already on the other side. My mind tells me that is a fact. But I have a feeling Núñez is in this country, our land of the Indians. Of course, I have frequently spoken of him, his healing and his teaching. I also have a sharp memory-picture of his appearance. I can clearly visualize him, just the way I saw him day after day, month after month. But beside that, I have a feeling that Núñez has not left us—that he is here."

Ara smiled as she looked at me. "Foolish, foolish man! Of course he is here! He has never left. He will never leave. This is his country. We are his people. His life has meant more to the Indians than anyone they have ever known. We have had powerful shamans, but never anyone like Núñez.

"This life of our village which is so beautiful and good and peaceful is all due to Núñez. That you and I can be so happy together is due to him. All the Indians now living in peace and security know this. The great good of his life will always be with us. It will never die. Thousands of years from now, the blessings of his goodness will still be here. He is eternal!"

As Ara spoke I knew that what she said was true and that perhaps only Ara could have seen this so clearly and said it so beautifully.

Fully a year passed after Núñez's return before we knew that he had landed at a place called Lisbon, Portugal, August 9, 1537. Fray José recorded all these dates.

It was August of 1538 when we heard this news. My memories of Núñez and his wonderful life were very clear and were with me always. I connected Núñez with Jesu-Cristo because they seemed to be the same kind of people. As I studied all about Jesu-Cristo, I felt I was learning what made Núñez like he was, and that the Great Spirit lived and worked through both of them.

My life with Ara was good beyond belief. Every day with her was a joyful experience. We still had no promise of a child, although both of us wanted children. My relations with Ara's family were the best. I felt they had great affection for me. I was really part of the family. Also I had made friends with the other villagers, who began coming to me with many of their problems.

Fray José fulfilled this function with most of the villagers who were baptized into his church. Fray José was a man of great understanding and compassion and helped in every way he could. He now made visits to other villages and began teaching in them. Three villages besides ours had built churches and had groups of people who were baptized.

Fray José had also brought to the village an animal that was new to the people. He called it *una vaca* (a cow). This had been Núñez's name for the large bison that roamed the plains. But Fray José's cow was very gentle and gave milk. She had been bred by a *toro* (bull) in San Miguél and Fray José was happy when she gave birth to a young female, which Fray José called *una becera* and who would one day be a milk-cow like her mother.

The mother gave a great deal of rich milk and Fray José distributed most of this through the village to small children who had been weaned from their mother's milk. This was the beginning of what later was to become a large number of cows in the village. Later Fray José also gave cows to the surrounding villages.

Chapter XVIII

The Irrepressible but Mortal Estevánico

Travel constantly took place between the many villages. Much of this was just social visiting between families and their kin and other friends. Naturally, no formal or regular messenger service existed. However, every visitor from another village always brought with him all the news he could gather. Once in a great while, Fray José received a written message, but he was the only one in the village of Zopa who did. Eventually all the interesting news became common property, generally by word of mouth.

In this way, messengers had brought us news of Viceroy Don Antonio de Mendoza attempting to organize an expedition led by Dorantes to what the Spaniards called the Seven Cities of Cíbola. Mendoza had bought many horses and spent much money. The expedition failed and we never heard why. Knowing Dorantes, I felt he simply did not want to go.

Next we heard that Mendoza was organizing an expedition to be guided by Estevánico, Dorantes' moorish slave who had accompanied Núñez all the way from the tuna fields to the land of the Ópatas and south to Culiacán. We heard that Dorantes had sold Estevánico to Mendoza, and that Mendoza was putting Fray Marcos de Nisa in charge of the expedition to Cíbola.

The people of Cíbola were my people, although I had never been beyond the cities of the river the Spaniards called *el Río Grande del Norte* and that we called the Tiguex. However, I knew much about all these cities of the Pueblos, as the Spaniards called them. None of them was warlike.

The people were all farmers, raising mainly corn, beans, and calabashes. They had domesticated wild turkeys, using them largely for their feathers. They were peace-loving and fought only in defense of their homes. The language of the Seven Cities was different from ours on the River Tiguex. Nevertheless, most of our customs were alike.

A messenger arrived on the 12th day of March in the year 1539, saying that the expedition had left San Miguél in the province of Culiacán on March the 9th.

I had always liked Estevánico. He was cheerful, friendly and talkative. What he liked the most was to make love to the Indian women. And although sometimes the Spaniards had been so **crowded with the sick that even Estevánico had to make the sign** of the cross and pray over the sick, I knew he was nothing like Núñez in the desire to help and serve people.

The exploration party to Cíbola arrived at our village on March 15. Fray Marcos and Fray José greeted each other, having known each other before. The Estevánico I saw swaggering through the village was a different person from the carefree, pleasure-loving person I had known who traveled with Núñez. Now he carried a gourd decorated with feathers of red and white. The gourd was filled with pebbles. He rattled the gourd constantly. These gourd rattles were considered good luck charms, and even sacred to some of the people.

He wore gaudy green and red feathers decorating his arms and legs. Bells were attached to his silver anklets and bracelets. A crown of bright green parrot plumes adorned his head. He was normally a tall man, but his crown made him look seven feet high! He strutted when he walked. He felt he was endowed with supernatural powers. He tinkled every time he moved! He was arrogant and demanding.

That night before I could go to sleep, a series of clear memories passed through my mind. They were all about Estevánico and Núñez. I remembered the first time I had ever seen Estevánico at the feast of the tunas and how I had been envious of him because of his height. He had laughed and joked a great deal and I had admired him.

. . . When we had started on our journey westward, Estevánico was in daily contact with Núñez, who was always selfless and thinking of others while Estevánico thought only of himself and the gratification of his own physical desires. I recalled the times **Núñez reprimanded him because of the trouble he was causing** with the married men, constantly seeking the amorous favors of their wives. While Estevánico had begun to be more careful, evidently none of Núñez's ideals of service to others had any effect on him.

Then, when the number of multitudes had grown so great, Estevánico had been pressed into service and had been involved in the healing process. But none of the real spirit of Núñez had ever had any meaning to him! I relived all of this before I could go to sleep . . .

The party spent only one night in our village. The following morning I watched them leave. Estevánico strutted at the head of a large number of Indians. The gaudy feathers on his arms and legs fluttered in the wind. The bells on his wrists and ankles tinkled as he walked. He was followed by two large Spanish greyhounds. He was served by a company of young Indian women, who carried plates painted a brilliant green, off of which he ate. And it was well known that he slept with a different Indian woman every night.

I was invited to join Fray Marcos and Fray José as they visited. Fray Marcos seemed to have the wrong ideas about the Zuñi and the Pueblos. I heard him say, "We know there is much silver and gold there, and cities larger than the City of Mexico."

Because I wanted him to know the truth, I said, "Someone has told you wrong. These cities are the cities of my people. It is true that some of them are large and that they have houses of stone and clay that are sometimes five or six stories high. But these cities are not rich. They have no gold nor silver. They are farmers, growing corn, cotton, beans, and calabashes. Their clothes are made of cotton or the skins of animals, even as the people of this village you are now in. I told all this to Núñez!"

Fray Marcos did not receive this news well, although he remained polite. At that point it was easy for me to see that he did not want to hear the truth. But I had done what I could to help him know exactly how the Pueblos were.

"Your Estevánico is an arrogant man," Fray José told Fray Marcos.

"Yes, I know that. Yet Mendoza has given me absolute authority over him, and he must obey me on threat of serious punishment if he does not."

After they had left, Fray José said to me, "I do not envy Fray Marcos' responsibility for this expedition. I fear the expedition will fail. All of it seems wrong to me." We heard only the vaguest news of their northward progress.

Ara had observed Estevánico closely while he was in our village. "It is very strange," she said.

"What is strange?"

"This Estevánico traveled with Núñez these many, many moons over long miles, and yet none of Núñez's spirit is in Estevánico. How could a man be with the Child of the Sun day after day and not catch his spirit?"

"No," I said, "Estevánico was never like Núñez, nor Castillo, nor Dorantes. Estevánico has always sought only his own pleasure. Now he feels that he is somebody great, whom others should serve. He did not understand Núñez at all!"

Fray Marcos had said that Núñez had brought word of the Seven Cities and their wealth. Yet, knowing how accurate Núñez was in all his reports, I was sure that someone had exaggerated or twisted what he said. Núñez, of course, had never visited the Pueblo country. As I said, I had told him all about it. I had told him of the size of the Pueblos, some of which were large. Also I had described the many-storied houses and told him that the people were farmers, having no riches.

When I told Fray José this, he said, "Núñez could never have given a false report. This expedition is for political reasons. The governor wants to believe there is wealth there. No good will

come of any of it. Fray Marcos will bring back the report the
governor wants to hear. I wouldn't be surprised if the governor
has already told him what report to make!"

It was hard for me to accept at first that even the best of men
could be used for evil purposes. But later, in view of all that happened, I had to accept this. My knowledge of Núñez and my faith
in his total goodness and truthfulness made me reluctant to
believe that his report of Cíbola could be so twisted and exaggerated and used for ugly purposes. And yet it had been!

We did not hear the complete story of the expedition until Fray
Marcos returned from his long journey many months later. He
stopped only for the night in our village to stay with Fray José.

Before dark, Ara and I had asked the two priests to eat with us.
We wanted to share our food with them and we wanted to hear
about the expedition. Ara broiled fresh fish I had caught in the
river. She made *pinole* that tasted better than any I ever ate. She
also served hot tortillas and well-seasoned beans which Fray
José called *frijoles*. Well-cooked and seasoned calabash topped
off the meal. I knew that no one in the village could prepare such
tasty food as Ara.

As we ate in front of our lodge under the ramada, it took only
one comment from Fray José to get Fray Marcos talking. "We
want to hear all about your journey," said Fray José.

Fray Marcos started, "We stayed together until we arrived at
Vacupa. Then I made a serious mistake. Since I wanted to find
out about the Indians of the islands, I told Estevánico to go
ahead and scout out the country toward the Seven Cities. All the
Indians of the north inquired about Núñez. They could never
hear enough about him. And they all talked frequently about
him.

"Independence was what Estevánico was waiting for. He
wanted to be free of me. He felt he was a god. Many Indians
traveled in his company and a number of women waited on him
day and night. I tried, but there was nothing I could do about
this.

"I told him to send me back a small cross if he heard good news
of Cíbola. If the news was better the cross was to be twice the size
of his hand. If the news of Cíbola was very good he was to send

a messenger back with a very big cross.

"Estevánico started sending back only the very big crosses, so I felt the outlook for our visit to Cíbola was favorable.

"I talked with many Indians from the islands. They reported very large pearls, but they had none to show me. They wore necklaces of mother-of-pearl that were very pretty. These were the Seri Indians.

"The Tuesday after Passion Sunday, I left Vacupa. I continued getting from messengers who came back very large crosses from Estevánico.

"As I journeyed northward I stayed in Indian villages each night and was always entertained well with ample food and a comfortable lodge in which to sleep. One very pleasant town was at the confluence of two rivers.* Even in the north the Indians kept asking about Núñez.

"Everywhere I went there was news of the great cities farther to the north, reporting vessels of gold and silver and much turquoise. I saw turquoise necklaces in every village I visited, and was told that they all came from Cíbola and that even the doors of the houses there were decorated with turquoise."

As he paused I said, "Yes, the Pueblos have some turquoise, but no silver and gold, which are soft metals my people have never found useful."

"But there were in the villages reports of gold and silver almost everywhere I went," Fray Marcos said defensively.

"Many of these Indians exaggerate greatly," I answered. "They tell you what you want to hear, not what is really the truth."

Fray Marcos did not answer. I could see pride in Ara's eyes as she looked at me.

"A messenger came with a very big cross and the news that Estevánico now had with him 300 people. So I drew nearer to Cíbola. At one village where I stayed the headman had some five or six chains of turquoise about his neck.

"Then came the bad day. The son of a chief had gone with

* The Gila River and the Colorado River

Estevánico. He returned nearly exhausted, his face covered with sweat, and fear in his voice.

"This man said that when Estevánico was within a day's journey of Cíbola, he sent messengers ahead, saying that he was coming to heal their sick and that he represented a white man who would soon follow him. He gave the messenger his sacred gourd decorated with feathers and a string of bells. Estevánico also made demands of the city's treasures and the use of their women. The message that he sent was not one that would please the people of Cíbola.

"When the lord of Cíbola received the sacred gourd and the demands, he went into a rage and threw them violently on the ground. He told the messenger that he had no desire to see his master, nor to accede to any of his demands, and that the doors of the city would in no way be opened to him.

"When Estevánico's messenger returned to him, Estevánico made light of this message of resistance. He told his people that all the villages accepted him and gave him gifts and that this unfriendly answer meant nothing. 'When I get there, they will receive me gladly,' he said.

"So Estevánico proceeded to Cíbola. He was met by armed men outside the city and taken to a great house some distance from the city. There he and a number of his people were held prisoner without food or water.

"Early in the morning the chief's son who brought us the news, feeling great thirst, had slipped past the guard who was dozing and went to the small creek to drink. Here, hidden by willows, he made the decision not to return to the house. He watched from his screen of willows and large rocks, and observed all that happened.

"After the sun came up, he saw armed men approaching the house. Estevánico and those inside started running out of the house.

"Arrows killed several of these people. The chief's son did not see Estevánico shot, but he felt sure he had been killed since not one of those who ran escaped. It seems all were killed.

"The greatest part of Estevánico's company had stayed far away from the city and had already turned back, returning to their own country. This son of a chief who brought the message stayed close to Cíbola, hidden until dark when it was safe for him to come back to us.

"Now among the people around me there was much lamentation, since those who had been killed were kin to some of them, and others were friends," Fray Marcos continued.

"All the former hospitality to me disappeared. Yet I wanted to get sight of this city and told the people of my determination. At first none of them was going with me. But when they saw I was going on alone, two of their leaders said they would accompany me.

"The three of us journeyed toward Cíbola. We finally came to the crest of a hill overlooking the plain and the city. I saw the size of the place, that it was very large, and I saw the stone houses of many levels.

"After I had seen it, I decided to go no nearer, since their anger might be dangerous. The three of us retraced our steps. Now I traveled as quickly as I could, because nowhere were the Indians as friendly and receptive as they had been. So now I am here, on my way back to Culiacán."

Both Ara and I had listened intently to all of Fray Marcos' account. We discussed it fully before we slept. It was then that I made up my mind to tell Fray José what I believed was the truth about Fray Marcos' story.

The next morning Fray Marcos left us to return to Culiacán. He said his next job was to write up a report of the expedition. I later read that report and found what I had expected, that Fray Marcos de Nisa had magnified all the inaccurate rumors about the fabulous treasures of gold and silver in the cities of Cíbola.

When Fray José and I were alone, I said to him, "Fray José, there is a serious falsehood in this story of Fray Marcos."

Fray José said, "I am not surprised. This man believes every rumor. Also he wants to make a favorable report to the government, hoping it will benefit him. This makes for a distortion of the truth. But tell me how you know there is a falsehood."

"It takes no magician to know this. I know how far it is to Cíbola. This is the hot time of the year, when travel must be slow. Through the hot country, which is like desert, the traveler can advance only in the cool morning, or after the sun gets low. To have made the trip back from Zuñi in the time he claimed, he would have had to cover about 30 miles a day through desert and rough country. No sane man would make this claim and expect to be believed!*

"Fray Marcos claims to have made this trip faster than a person can travel in cool weather. He never saw Cíbola at all! He has made all this up to create an impression that he thinks will make him look good."

Fray José thought about what I said for a few minutes. "You are right. No one could have made this trip in the short time Fray Marcos claims. There is no truth in his claims to have seen Cíbola."

* Carl Sauer, *Sixteenth Century North America*, Berkeley, Calif.: University of California Press, 1971, p. 127.

Chapter XIX
The Golden One
and the Servant

"Whatever is based on falsehood," said Fray José, "is destined for failure. Fray Marcos is taking a false report to the viceroy."

Naturally, I was much concerned about the expedition to the Pueblos, because the village of my people was there. While I had never visited the Seven Cities of Cíbola, I had known about them for many years.

What Fray Marcos was picturing as seven large cities of great wealth were seven villages of moderate size, having neither silver nor gold, some turquoise, and composed chiefly of farmers raising corn, beans, and squash. They were peace-loving, fighting only to defend themselves if threatened.

There were many Pueblos, some of them with large numbers of people. Farther to the north were the Pueblos later to be called the Hopis. Here, even though they were in a colder climate, they raised cotton. The period of growth for plants was short, but the strain of cotton they raised matured quickly. Their cotton was much in demand and made a good item of trade.

Fray José told me, "The viceroy feels that he needs to find new cities which are rich so that he can send ships loaded with treasure to the king. Therefore, any hint of riches planted in his mind finds a fertile field. The viceroy is quick to believe and magnify such a report."

True to Fray José's prediction, Viceroy Mendoza seized Fray Marcos' exaggerated report eagerly and began to act upon it. The rumor of treasure-cities in the north spread all over Mexico. It was a contagious fever. This was what the people were eager to hear!

The governor of New Galicia was Francisco Vásquez Coronado. It was he that Mendoza finally selected to explore the Pueblos. But first Melchior Diaz was asked to scout out the country to find the best route for Coronado to take. Through our village of Zopa he came with fifteen horsemen and a number of Indians.

Here he stopped to visit with Fray José, who told him, "I have here with me a man who was born and spent his early life in the Pueblos. You will probably remember him since he went to Culiacán with Álvar Núñez Cabeza de Vaca."

Melchior Diaz visited long with me, learning about life in the Pueblos. Much later I read his report and most of it was correct. One written statement was ridiculous: he reported cannibalism among the Pueblos. As far back as tribal memory goes, there has been a taboo among my people against eating human flesh.

Then Diaz proceeded up the route that Cabeza de Vaca had traveled, except he went to the Mogollon Rim of the Colorado Plateau, from which he departed because of the severity of the cold. A number of his southern Indians, unaccustomed to such low temperatures, died of exposure. Diaz returned and met Coronado with information about Cíbola at Chiametla in southern Sinaloa.

The advance party of Coronado's expedition passed through Zopa in May of 1540. It was a large expedition. Coronado, at its head, rode into Zopa just as the bright rays of the western sun struck his company. I found myself wishing it was Núñez going to the Pueblos. Then the people would be helped. Now they would be in danger.

Coronado was on a beautiful horse, as black and shiny as smooth obsidian. Ara and I stood hand-in-hand to watch his dramatic passing. His armor was gold-plated, as was his helmet, with three bright golden feathers in it. I thought I had never seen any man look more majestic. He sat on his horse, erect and graceful. Coronado did not spend the night in Zopa since he wanted to use all the remaining light of the day to get as far north as possible.

I know it was a vision, but right after seeing the splendor and physical power of Coronado, I saw Núñez. He was afoot. His tall, slender frame was without clothing, except for the usual breechclout. He was bending over a pallet on which lay an Indian who was obviously sick. Núñez's healing hands were stretched out touching the prone body. It was so real it took my breath away. I blinked my eyes and opened them. As suddenly as it had come, the vision was gone! But I had a feeling I had seen my teacher as he really was, a man of unusual inner power.

Núñez had no armor, no cutlass, no spear. About him there had been no glitter, no ostentation. There had been nothing impressive about him physically. But now, while the sudden vision had vanished, I remembered his large brown eyes, radiant with inner light. I remembered his concern for everyone that needed help.

And I knew that, even though Núñez and I had parted, he would always be with me, no matter where I was or where he was. The magic of his inner power, his love, his great compassion, meant that in the most powerful way, he would always be there—my teacher, my guide, the one who had given me my first real knowledge of the Great Spirit in the life of man.

That night, Fray José came to my lodge. "Uri, you have seen an exhibition of the pride of Spain."

"I have never seen a more impressive-looking man, with the western sun glittering on his golden armor, Fray José. It was a glorious sight!"

"It is not the outward appearance that makes any man great. When I first saw Núñez, he was as naked as any savage of the wilderness. Yet he had an inner greatness that needed no gold-covered armor, nor proud prancing horse with arched neck to make any impression. Long ago, Jesu-Cristo said, 'Whosoever would be chief among you, let him be your servant.' Núñez had learned to be the servant of mankind. Have you ever heard the story of *El Dorado* (the Golden One)?"

I told Fray José I had not.

"It comes from South America, probably from Peru. Tremendous treasures of gold and silver were taken back to Spain from that country. The main thought in the minds of nearly all the Spaniards was of riches. They were avaricious, greedy for great wealth. So the legend of *El Dorado* was believed. As Mendoza and Coronado, the explorers believed what they wanted to believe.

"There was a kingdom, said the Indians, so rich that the king in certain ceremonies was covered with oil and then sprinkled with gold dust. Then he washed himself in the lake and many others threw gold objects in the lake. He became a golden man later, symbolizing all the greed and lust of the Spaniards for gold. There were for years numerous expeditions that went out looking for the kingdom so rich in gold that their king was frequently coated with gold dust . . . So began the legend of *El Dorado*, the Golden One."

For a long time Fray José was silent.

Finally I said, "So we have seen *El Dorado*, the Golden One."

"I fear that we have, Uri. This expedition is much the same as the others, especially the reasons for it. Francisco Vásquez Coronado—young, handsome, with wavy brown hair and blue eyes, sitting gracefully on his black horse, clad in his gold-plated armor—is a symbol of the lust of Spain for gold, silver, gems or any other treasure. This lust leads them to impose upon or even slaughter anyone or any group who gets in their way. It leads them to expect those whom they conquer to feed them and house them. And if they find any treasure of gold or silver or any other kind, they will take it."

"All they will find in the Pueblos are a few turquoise."

"Then you may be sure they will rob the people of these. There are over a thousand men in Coronado's party. They will quickly impoverish any Indian village they pass through."

"I fear for my people, Fray José. They will be the victims of this expedition. I only wish it were Núñez, going to heal and to teach."

"Yes, if the conquest goes to the village of your people, they will be ruined. The greedy Spanish conquistador carries the seeds of ruin and destruction in his heart and mind. Coronado is not a bloodthirsty man, but he is part of a system that destroys everything in its path."

One of the Cáhita men of our village, a very strong, adventurous, young man by the name of Plara, about 20 years old, joined the large number of Indians who accompanied Coronado. He was in the personal service of one of Coronado's lieutenants, and it was from him several years later that I was given the full story of what happened during the expedition.

I shall try as accurately as possible to relate briefly what he told me:

Coronado found almost everything quite different from what Fray Marcos had told him. There were rough mountains that took many days to pass through; Fray Marcos had said that the way would be smooth and easy. Food supplies which they had expected from the villages amounted to almost nothing. In the land of the Ópatas food was scarce because of extended drought, except for a common cactus food called *la pitahaya* and the roasted hearts of the *maguey*. Afterward there was a desert to cross where both food and water were scarce. There was hardship. There was thirst. There was extreme hunger.

The first to return from the expedition, however, was not Plara, but an armed party which had left Zuñi, as the Ópatas called it. (The name my people had for it was Hawikuh.) Fray Marcos was with this party and, as I later learned, had been sent back to Mexico City in disgrace because all his reports about the country had been false. As Fray Marcos came through Zopa, he had little to say. They had left Hawikuh around the first of August, 1540.

It was when our Cáhita man, Plara, later returned to Zopa that he gave us the full account of everything that he knew. There had been fighting at Hawikuh. Coronado had courageously led an attack of foot soldiers as they assaulted the houses from which the Indians had shot arrows, one of which had lodged in Coronado's foot. Coronado had also been hit with several rocks; but the crossbows and harquebuses of the Spaniards had finally routed the Indians, who fled the town—which was much smaller than Fray Marcos had reported. The Spaniards had found ample food, which was their greatest need. They found stores of maize and beans, and many turkeys. They found houses of several stories made not of stone, but of a combination of clay and stone. The rooms were small. Even the reports of many turquoise were false. There were only a few of the blue stones. Coronado sent out exploring parties in several directions, because he wanted to find anything of value in reach.

Captain Alvarado was appointed to ride to the east to explore that region. He sent back an interesting report. He had discovered a large river. He estimated that there were eighty towns in the river country, one of which was a **very** large city,* numbering around 15,000 inhabitants. The people were peaceful at first, more interested in agriculture than war. Alvarado invited Coronado and the entire expedition to spend the winter on the Rio Grande (the Tiguex), to which he gave a name of his choice—*el Rio de Guadalupe.*

General Coronado accepted this invitation. Later he was followed by the main army. Coronado forced my people to abandon one complete town in order to house his army. He levied a forced assessment of clothes from the villagers so his men could remain warm. This was too heavy a burden for my people to bear, since it meant that many of them would suffer from the cold.

One of the women of a village had been raped, and nothing was done about it. Later it became common knowledge that this had been the crime of a man high in the favor of Mendoza. It seemed that Coronado finally had fifteen hundred men, a thousand horses, five hundred cattle, and five hundred sheep. The river villages could not support this added number of hungry stomachs. Naturally, my people became hostile and angry.

The Pueblos discovered that the Spaniards were vulnerable and that their horses were the most vulnerable. They began to defy the Spaniards in many ways. All of this informed the

* Taos

Spaniards that the Pueblos of the Rio Grande were no longer submissive. The Spaniard was the invader of a domain that was rightfully that of the peaceful Pueblos. The Pueblos had a right to resist.

One of the most obvious acts of defiance had been against the Spaniards' horses. The Indians stole a number of these and killed them.

Coronado had held a council of war in which he and his leaders decided on military assault of the Pueblos. They started in my home village which they called Arenal. They overwhelmed the small garrison, killing many Pueblos and capturing many. They burned a number of these captives while they were still alive, at the stake. What became of my family, I shall never know. They might have been among those burned alive, or they might have been killed in battle. At best they were driven out of their homes in midwinter during a snowstorm . . .

When I heard this from Plara, it was long after it had occurred. I was brokenhearted to learn that the worst had happened to my family. Fray José was grieved, too. Ara wept when she heard of the destruction of my people.

Fray José said, "I knew something like this was bound to happen. The very nature of the expedition was for the Spaniards to exploit the people of the Pueblos. That the Pueblos should resent this and defy them speaks well for the Pueblos."

Plara had told us further that the Spaniards besieged one of the larger Pueblos, Moho. The people, forced to suffer extreme thirst, had tried to escape. The Spaniards slaughtered many of them as they fled. Most of those who managed to escape froze to death in the severe cold. The weather was cold enough to freeze the Tiguex River solid from bank to bank.

Other Pueblos were then attacked. Some were burned. The neighboring towns were all abandoned. This was the tragedy that befell my people as a result of the lust of Spaniards for treasure and power.

I remembered Núñez quoting a verse from his *Biblia*, "Lay not up for yourselves treasures on earth, where moth and rust doth corrupt, and thieves break through and steal; but lay up for yourselves treasures in heaven, where neither moth nor rust can corrupt, nor thieves break through and steal, for where your treasure is, there will your heart be also." I repeated this verse to Fray José.

He said, "Núñez had learned the meaning of this verse, but few other Spaniards have. Fray Marcos, for all his sanctimonious pretense, has not. And from what Plara tells us, the other priests of the expedition urged Coronado to attack the Pueblos. And we call ourselves holy men! How different it would have been if Núñez had gone to your people!"

Plara told us about Coronado's long and vain quest for treasure in the land of Quivira, far to the northeast of the Pueblos. Returning from Quivira, Coronado suffered a serious fall from his horse due to the breaking of a rotted leather cinch of his saddle. Before having recovered sufficiently to begin the return journey, news reached him from Sonora that the peaceful Ópata Indians had finally rebelled because of their mistreatment by Alcaráz who had been commander of the garrison.

Knowing this man's record, and how Núñez had opposed him, I could not see why Alcaráz had been given this responsibility. He abused the Ópatas, using some of them as virtual slaves. He stole their wives. He was much worse than Estevánico.

The night he was killed, it was reported that he was sleeping with two Ópata women, whom he had forced into submission. They hated him and shot him with arrows poisoned with the famous *yerba pestífera*. Some of the Spaniards escaped during the uprising. Othere were killed with poisoned arrows. Not only had Alcaráz abused the Ópatas, he had freely permitted other Spanish soldiers to do the same.

"Good riddance!" commented Fray José when we heard of Alcaráz's death. He quoted a verse from his *Biblia*, "Vengeance is mine. I will repay, saith the Lord."

Coronado's return to Mexico was slow and tedious and painful. It was also dangerous, since the Ópatas were generally insurgent and some men of the expedition were shot with arrows poisoned with *la yerba pestífera*.

Coronado was carried in a litter. They left the Tiguex country in April, 1542. When the procession moved through our village, Ara and I saw Coronado on his litter. His face was pale and emaciated. This was the last of May, 1542. He left Culiacán for Compostela on June 24, 1542.

Seeing the pallid, gaunt face of Coronado, carried on his litter by four Nahuas, I thought back to the day when he rode ahead of his column on his prancing black horse, its coat glistening in the westering sun. I remembered his erect, graceful figure, clad in gold-plated armor, his blue eyes and wavy brown hair under a gold-coated helmet, decorated with three golden feathers. As I remembered him, an unusual beauty surrounded his courtly figure.

But immediately superimposed on this came a clear vision of Núñez, and the knowledge that his spirit was vastly different from that of the avaricious expedition and the physical arrogance and beauty of Coronado. I knew now that Núñez and I were not separated and would never be!

Fray José had his usual apt quotation from his *Biblia* after watching the almost funereal procession bearing Coronado's broken body on its litter. "Pride goeth before destruction, and a haughty spirit before a fall."

Chapter XX
A Night of Remembering

That night, Ara was needed in the lodge of one of her friends who had just delivered her first baby. Left alone, I was quick to discover that I needed the solitude.

It turned out to be a sleepless night. My mind was active. It was full of thoughts of my association with Núñez. Perhaps this was a continuation of my realistic vision of Núñez upon seeing Coronado on his stretcher. I began reliving my experiences with Núñez, starting with my first sight of him on a high bluff lookout as he gazed eastward toward the rolling country below him. I remembered kneeling before him spontaneously, and could feel again the touch of his hand on my head as he blessed me.

I reviewed those relaxing, beautiful days that followed in the month that we spent together in the wilderness. I was sure that, even so early in our friendship, Núñez sensed the importance of teaching me. That was the beginning of my new life!

Vividly, there returned to me the many scenes of healing in the village of the Avavares where we spent the winter. Had I not witnessed the results of the healing, it would have been hard for me to believe. Anyone reading *El Nuevo Testamento* of the miracles performed by Jesu-Cristo as he healed the sick might have the same difficulty in believing. How fortunate I was to have seen all that had happened through Núñez. The ministry of Núñez illumined for me the life and work and teaching of Jesu-Cristo.

I was amazed at the number of passages from *La Biblia* that Núñez knew from memory. When I expressed my surprise, Núñez had said to me, "When I was a soldier, I was away from home a great deal. I had much time on my hands. I always liked to read and I had a copy of *La Biblia* that had been translated into Spanish in 1509. I read it over and over again. While my understanding was limited, I knew many of the passages were very important and meaningful. I easily remembered what I read, so those significant passages remained in my mind. My understanding of them came gradually. The willingness of Jesu-Cristo to suffer death by cruel crucifixion, rather than fight his enemies, was the beginning of my dislike for violence and killing, and my decision not to follow the career of a soldier.

"But it took my misfortune on *La Isla del Malhado* and my misery during enslavement to really humble me, and to lead me to respect and love my fellow man. I saw how I could love even the most primitive men and even those who were my enemies."

I could hear Núñez's tone of voice as his words came back to me. It was almost as if he were right there speaking to me in person.

Many memories came to me as clear pictures. I saw all the details of our visit to the village of the Susolos, where the man who had been sick was pronounced dead. I saw Núñez and Dorantes as they examined him, felt for a pulse and found none. Again I heard Núñez as he forbade the villagers to cover the body with mats, and as he prayed over the man whose face was bloodless and his being apparently lifeless.

I remembered watching this still figure and later seeing the eyes flutter, the arms and legs begin to move, the body rising to a sitting position, as he asked for food. Again I heard the wild shouts of the people and heard my own voice raised exultantly. I did not understand it then, nor do I understand it now. I only know it happened. I saw it all happen and now, in memory, I was seeing it again. How privileged I was to have witnessed it. How could this and all those other astonishing things have happened?

Again I heard Núñez say, "I do not do the healing. *El Bendito Dios* does the healing through me and my simple prayers."

Jesu-Cristo had said almost the same thing! "The words that I speak unto you, I speak not of myself. But the Father, Who dwelleth in me, He doeth the works."*

Once more I seemed to hear Núñez say, "Jesu-Cristo told his followers, 'He that believeth in me, the works that I do shall he do also; and greater works than these shall he do, because I go unto my Father!'"**

Then Núñez went on to explain to me, "You know, Cazador, although I had read those words and remembered them, I had no idea what they meant. Then these wonders began to happen when I was almost forced to utter my simple prayers for healing and to go through my little ceremony. Do you think it was my words and my ceremony that accomplished the wonders? Never! It was the presence of *el Bendito Dios* that achieved those wonders!"

Next I found myself seeing again the great crowds thronging Núñez as we went northwest up the River of Nuts visiting village after village. I saw again the great excitement and joy of the people as they brought the sick to him for healing and as many sought only to touch him.

In my restlessness, I wandered outdoors into the moonless night, the sky a purplish black overhead, studded with brilliant stars. Far away I heard the lonely cry of a wolf. As I stood in the great stillness, I heard the long, drawn-out wail repeated and felt a kinship with this wild creature, both of us created by the Great Spirit.

As I gazed toward the stars, I whispered a prayer of thanksgiving for the distant stars, for the great world about me, its beauty and its life, and the life in me.

I returned to the lodge and lay on my mats, wide awake. As

* St. John 14:10
** St. John 14:12

before, memory would not be denied. Now I was beholding Núñez, with his crude obsidian knife and, greater than that, with his great courage and faith, as he successfully operated on the Indian in whose chest was lodged an arrowhead. And again, after this astounding operation, sick were brought to him by hundreds on stretchers from the piñon mountains.

My mind jumped to the village of the Jumano Indians, again with the great number of healings taking place. I recalled Núñez using the sign language to teach about his *Bendito Dios*.

There appeared to me next the multitude of sick that were healed in the Ópata villages. Quickly my mind went from this to the change in Núñez when he heard of the depredations of the Spanish slave-traders among the Indians of western Mexico.

He quickly became a man with one immediate goal: to free the west coast Indians from the inhumanity and barbarity of the Spaniards. Núñez, the bold champion of human rights!

Now I could understand the verse I had read in San Lucas, when Jesu-Cristo, just beginning his active ministry, pronounced these prophetic words in the synagogue: " . . . the Spirit of the Lord is upon me . . . he hath sent me to preach deliverance to the captives . . . to set at liberty them that are bruised."* This was exactly what Núñez was doing!

I visualized him as he stood firmly and erect, naked and unarmed, confronting Alcaráz on his powerful horse. Alcaráz was armed and armored. The big difference between them was that Núñez was in harmony with the Great Spirit, and Alcaráz was not. It was this that gave Núñez the final victory.

And because of this, the native people in western Mexico now lived free, no longer under threat of enslavement. In our village of Zopa we could live without fear, in peace and love because of what Núñez was and what he had done.

The whole night passed in wakefulness. I needed this time of clarification. Now birds began to twitter outside, and the gray light of dawn shined through the windows. I went outdoors with the conviction that I was completely committed to Núñez's way

* St. Luke 4:18

of life, and surer of my harmony with the Great Spirit.

As the sun came up, I breathed a prayer of thanksgiving for what my life had become because of Núñez. I found myself going through the beautiful ceremony of the Ópatas, as I reached out my hands to the light to fill them with it and bathe my body in it.

So ended this strange episode, from which I emerged knowing that within and without I was bathed with the light of the Great Spirit, as was Núñez, my leader and teacher.

Chapter XXI
An Important Letter that Changed My Life

When he had first come to Mexico, Fray José had studied the Nahua language in Mexico City. He told me that the Piman was kin to the Nahua and that I might as well learn Nahua.

"You have a gift for languages, Uri. Some day you will find a great use for this. I really have never seen anyone who could learn languages more quickly or better than you."

This made me feel good. It was more important to have this ability than to have long legs. Fray José had written to the fathers in Mexico City, asking them to send someone to help him in the village of Zopa and the surrounding country. This is how Atlan, a Nahua who had been educated in the schools of Pedro de Gante in Mexico City, happened to come to us. I think Fray José really sent for Atlan so that he could teach me the Nahua language.

Atlan was well acquainted with Pedro de Gante, who was now becoming quite an old man, although he was still in good health. "First Pedro de Gante started his school for Indians in Texcoco," Atlan explained to me. "Then in 1526 he changed the school to Mexico City and called it San José. It was connected with the convent of San Francisco. He gathered hundreds of Indian children to go to the school. He taught them arts and crafts, music, and reading. It is a fine school."

"Yes, my friend Guatél went to this school when he was just a stripling."

"Have you heard of the Colegio Mayór?"

"Yes, that is where Guatél is now going to school."

"It was started in 1540 and is greatly expanded. It will become a fine university some day."

"When you mentioned the date 1526, Atlan, I was made to remember that was two years before Núñez was cast up on the beach of the Island of Malhado."

Atlan had heard a great deal about Núñez, but he wanted to know firsthand the entire story. I spent hours telling him. I had repeated this story many, many times. It seemed as if it would have been monotonous. But it was not! I was always stimulated as I told of all the great things that Núñez had done.

After Atlan had been in Zopa about a month, all the village became excited. A messenger arrived on horseback from Culiacán bearing a letter. And it was for me! It was the first letter I had ever received in my life, written in Spanish on parchment, and from Núñez! This is still my most treasured possession.

Eagerly I read the letter, which said:

As you know, I have been desirous to return to Mexico. My heart is in Mexico with the Indians. But Hernando de Soto was appointed to the post that I wanted. I fear that his expedition will be like all other Spanish conquests, a search for power and riches and fame. This means the Indians will be abused. The thought of this angers me.

Never will I be able to get away from the responsiveness of the Indians to kindness, to healing, and to religious teaching. Those years of my journey toward Mexico are golden years in my memory. They were years of filling a need for thousands of Indians hungry for help. They were years of showing the love and power of God through healing and teaching. And to crown it came our victory over the forces of greed and avarice that had led to the enslave-

ment of countless Indians. If I had lived for only these experiences, my life would have been well spent.

But now I have received a difficult assignment from my king and shall soon be on my way to South America. In the colonies I shall govern, there has been gross injustice from every report I can get. The Indians have been abused and ravaged. Can I put a stop to all of this and institute justice and fair dealing? In my own strength I know this would be impossible, but God is all-powerful, so I shall go in His strength. If it can be done, it will be done through God's power and love.

You know my grief in not being able to return to Mexico and see again the countless people who love me. This would be heaven for me.

Know that I wish you well, Cazador. I know you and others in Mexico will carry on the good work.

I am affectionately your friend.

Álvar Núñez Cabeza de Vaca

All of Zopa gathered to hear my translation of the letter into the Piman language. When I finished reading, most of the villagers were wiping away their tears. Then they had me read it again!

I immediately sat down to answer this letter. I had no parchment, so I wrote on soft deerskin as clearly as I could.

Here is part of what I wrote:

As much as we wish you were returning to us, perhaps the need for you is greater in South America. As you go there to serve, you know that our prayers and best wishes go with you.

Even though you will be far to the south of us, did you know you are also here with us? Everybody in the Cáhita country honors and loves you. They all acknowledge that the freedom, peace and security we have here in Mexico is because of your influence as you stood firmly for human rights, justice and freedom and stopped the vicious practice of enslavement of the Indians. Now we peacefully grow our gardens, fish, hunt, dance and sing with a joy that we would not have if you had not come to liberate us.

*Not only in Cáhitaland, but even in remote villages in
the mountains you are honored and praised for the blessings you have brought everywhere.*

*The same is true among the Ópatas, and from what we
hear back in the wilderness country beyond the Ópatas.*

*And while we are too far to receive any word from them,
I am sure the same holds true among the Sumas, the
Jumanos, and the numerous tribes of the piñon-pine
country in the mountains. I believe that everywhere you
went the conversation around the campfires is about the
hope and joy you brought by your healing and teaching.
This goes all the way back to the Susolos and the
Avavares, where we spent that memorable winter and I
began the serious study of the Spanish language.*

*No, we are not separated from you. We are one with you
just as we are all one with the Great Spirit. So real is your
presence among us that some have said they have actually
seen you. Whether this is true or not, you are here in reality, in your spirit and your influence. And as one whom I
know well keeps telling me, you are here forever!*

The village insisted that I read them my letter, which I did in
translation to the Piman. The people were all seated as I read.
No one stirred or coughed. There was almost complete silence.

When I finished reading everyone in one motion sprang to his
feet and shouted. Then they embraced each other and danced
with joy. What a beautiful time it was!

About a month later, Fray José received a letter which he read
to me. The part that was important said, "You have been appointed Professor of Theology in the Colegio Mayór. We would
like for you to come back to Mexico City as soon as you can to
take up these duties. A replacement will be sent to your mission
in Zopa."

Soon afterward Fray José called me into his lodge. "Uri, I want
you to go to Mexico City with me. Your gift with languages can
be helpful in the college, and you can have an interesting, useful
life. I am sure you will become a teacher. Ara can go to school,
too, since they have classes for Indian women in Mexico City.
Atlan will stay here at Zopa until my replacement comes. Or if

he wishes, he may stay longer."

This, of course, came as a great surprise to me. That I, Uri, the dwarf, the trader, could go to a college to learn many things and that I could become a teacher seemed a world completely apart from my former life. Of course, I had known since my visit back home to Senecú that my life was to be vastly different from that of a trader. Even then I had a feeling I should become a teacher.

I talked this over with Ara, and with her mother and father. They all agreed that this would be an unusually good opportunity for both Ara and me. I thought with regret of leaving the peaceful life of Zopa and all our loving friends.

Within weeks Fray José, Ara, and I were riding toward Mexico City. It was a long and interesting journey.

For the first time I saw the Pacific Ocean. We went through Mazatlán and saw its long beaches with their hard-packed sand. We turned southeast through low mountains as we rode toward Guadalajara.

For the first time I saw a volcano, a smoking mountain. This lay to the east of the trail to Guadalajara. There were long beds of lava which had once been molten rock from the volcano, which Fray José told me was only a small one. The road across the lava flow was rough and slow.

After many weeks of travel we came to the high plateau country of Mexico City. It was green and cool. As we came into the city, Fray José told me, "Now you are in the land where money is needed. Fortunately, I shall see to it that you have a place close to the college in which to live. You can live with me first and later have a house of your own. We will call you our gardener. There is another gardener who will do all the work. We will call Ara our cook, but again there is a cook who will do all the work. You and Ara will both go to school. You will become very well-educated people."

Fray José and three other priests lived in a long, low, stone house. Ara and I had two rooms to ourselves.

"The air here is like the air in the village at the crest of the mountain where I first met you," Ara commented to me as we first entered the city.

I learned that this city was high, seven thousand feet above the level of the sea.

"Look at the good view we have of Popocatepetl and Ixtaccihuatl." Ara looked through one of our windows with me at the two distant snow-covered peaks.

"It is a beautiful place, Uri. We shall have a good life here. You are now finding what you are supposed to do. You have great gifts."

This was the true beginning of my life as a scholar and teacher. Actually, of course, it had really taken root with Núñez, when I met him overlooking the eastern pine forests and when he began to teach me Spanish and the wonders of the written word. Realizing that a man with the spirit of Núñez always brings about betterment in the lives of the people he touches, I planned to begin my life as a scholar and later as a teacher holding Núñez as my pattern and my ideal. And I knew I would be true to this ideal. What I had from Núñez was permanent and would never leave me.

Chapter XXII

Guatél Tells Us about his Encounter with the Slave-Hunters

The day after we moved in, Guatél came by to see us. He was his usual smiling self and gave us a good feeling as he welcomed us.

"I want to hear all about what happened after you left Zopa on my mule. By the way, where is my little mule?"

Guatél grinned. "Have you ever eaten mule meat? It is delicious, and nourishing, too!" He laughed contagiously. "Look," he said, "I am finishing a paper for one of my professors. It has to be in by tomorrow. Let me come tomorrow and bring Maria, my beautiful wife, and I'll tell you everything."

This was a new Guatél! I had always known his possibilities but maybe I had underestimated him.

In the afternoon of the next day, Guatél came with Maria.

"You were right," I said to him.

"How do you mean?"

"She is beautiful!" Maria was a Nahua girl with hair so black that it was almost unbelievable. Her large brown eyes were alive and observant. She smiled and curtsied to me after my remark.

"Have you become a Catholic?" I asked him.

"No, and you know why. Have you?"

"No, for the same reason. The life of Jesu-Cristo has great beauty in it and great good. Through the example of Núñez I have let Jesu-Cristo become my teacher and guide. But I, the same as you, can't accept all that the church teaches," I told him. "I want to hear everything that happened after you left Zopa on my little mule."

So Guatél began his story. "Before I begin to tell you all that happened, I want to say again that Núñez was the greatest man I've ever known. That he did not succeed in freeing that large group of slaves, although it was disappointing to me, in no way diminishes his greatness. In the same way Jesu-Cristo refused to use arms, or force, or his ability to perform miracles when he was tried and condemned and put to death on the cross.

"Núñez believed implicitly in the way of Jesu-Cristo. Núñez used all the power he could muster to free the slaves, and failed. I have never known any man who had the spiritual strength of Núñez. He had great magnetism, too. Look at your loyalty and love for him."

"Not only Uri," said Ara. "All the Indians where Núñez went love him and recognize his goodness and the freedom he gave us."

"That is true," answered Guatél. "Perhaps it was my background as a boy that made me run away from the sight of the slaves. I remembered how my mother and father were in chains, and beaten and starved, and finally killed. I could no longer stand to see the abuse of the slaves. So I returned to Zopa. That night I could not sleep. First, I felt like a coward because I had run away! And during the night, I came to the conclusion there was something I could do. Let me tell you how I reasoned.

"I like the coyote, or as Maria calls them in Nahua, *coyotl*. I usually would not kill a coyote. I like to see them run wild and free. But once I saw one foaming at the mouth and staggering. I knew he had rabies. I killed him without compunction, knowing that it would keep other animals from being bitten and getting rabies.

"I know the way I chose was not Núñez's way. But I looked on the slave-traders as I did that mad coyote. So, during the night I laid my plan. I knew I had to do it. And may it be the last time I ever have to do anything like it!

"I rode your mule to Culiacán. I had a little Spanish money with me. I traded the mule and all my money for a good fast horse. I rode the horse toward Compostela." Guatél paused to get a drink.

When he came back I said, "I have just received a book from Spain. Before Núñez left for South America he must have left instructions with the publisher at Valladolid to send me a copy of his *Relación*. When I have finished it, I'll pass the copy around."

Guatél expressed interest in Núñez's book and wanted to read it as soon as possible. He then continued his story.

"I quickly overtook the slave-hunters and their captives. Because of the sickness and the starvation of the captives, their travel was quite slow. Later I found out that Núñez's armed escort had grown impatient and hurried on to Compostela.

"As you know, I had my best bow and a number of good arrows. Also I had ample poison in a small, thick leather pouch in which I always carried it. The Spaniards call it *la yerba pestífera*.

"There were six Spanish slave-hunters. The first night after I overtook them I left my horse tied to a tree some distance from their camp and scouted to find out how their camp was situated.

"The Spaniards built a fire off to themselves, away from where the captives lay in their chains. One Spaniard guarded the captives. And they changed guards every three hours.

"It was an easy matter for me to get close to this guard. I was only fifty paces from him when I sent my first poisoned arrow home. The wretch fell heavily to the ground without even a groan. The poison kills fast! After I had killed him I remembered how he or another had used a lash on Núñez when he protected a slave.

"I did not wait until they found him, but went back to my horse and slept for several hours. And I thanked the Great Spirit that my arrow had gone straight and true.

"After resting, I returned to the camp. The Spaniards, now afraid, slept away from their fire and out of sight. The new guard must have kept his distance from any light. So I went back and slept until before dawn.

"I awakened and stole back to the camp of the Spaniards. They were cooking their breakfast in the dim light. I saw well enough so that I shot one by the fire. After the man fell, two of his companions with those silly harquebuses mounted their horses and rode out in my direction.

"That was exactly what I was hoping for. From my hiding place I knocked one off his horse. The other turned to run and I hit him in the back. With that *veneno*, one scratch will kill a person. I was taking no chances. I shot my arrows hard and deep.

"That accounted for four of the six in short order. I was determined to get them all. As I said, I looked on them as I would have at rabid coyotes.

"The remaining two mounted their horses and rode away as fast as they could. That left their captives without a single guard. I didn't think the two frightened guards who fled would come back. Yet there was always danger."

Ara and I had sat spellbound by Guatél's tale, partly because we so closely identified with the captives in chains.

Guatél continued, "My next job was to free the prisoners from those bloodstained chains, a hard job. I had brought along a good file which I had sense enough to pick up in Culiacán. The first thing I did was to cut loose four of the strongest looking men and post them as guards in four directions. Then, finding a key on one of the dead Spaniards, I was able to unlock the chains and free every one of those half-starved people.

"I caught two of the dead Spaniards' horses and let the weakest prisoners ride them. One of them was a fine saddlehorse. My next job was to get food. First, I made the freed prisoners walk to a creek not far away and drink the good, clear water. Next, those who wished to clean themselves, and who were not sick, bathed in the creek. Then I posted guards and went after a deer. Fortunately, I killed one in an hour. I took the meat to the creek and let the people start cooking.

"Then I told them I had a job to do. I saw several of them smile for the first time. They knew what I was going to do.

"By now it was late in the afternoon. I picked up the trail of the two guards easily and followed it until dark. It was the road to Compostela, so I followed it even after dark until I was tired out.

"I slept until dawn and after cooking a piece of venison I had brought, I went back to tracking the guards. I kept well behind them, since I didn't want to risk an encounter.

"At night they built a fire and I waited until they were eating and then I crept up close and shot two more poisoned arrows before they could know that danger was near. Both of my arrows sank deep in their bodies.

"I left them there for the buzzards. I shot those six men without hatred. The earth is not big enough for men like those.

"The next day I returned with the horses to my freed captives. 'My job of killing mad coyotes is done,' I told them. They laughed and some patted my shoulder.

"They told me of a village that was on higher ground about five leagues away, so we put the sickest on the horses and went to this village. Here the freed prisoners were able to find help. And here I left them, no longer feeling like the coward I did when I saw you at Zopa. I sold the horses in Compostela. No one asked any questions. I rode the fifth horse, the best one, here to Mexico City and sold him. Then I got a job as a *mozo* (manservant) taking care of the yard of a rich family. I still work for them so that Maria and I can live. I can work and go to school, too. Life here is good and we are happy.

"Since I speak Nahua, I made many friends among the people of this beautiful language. That was how I came to know Maria. Her family was glad to get rid of her, especially since she was marrying a rich *mozo*!"

Maria's laughter was like music as we all laughed together.

We saw much of Guatél and Maria after that. And many times our visits were dominated by discussion of Núñez, his healing, his teaching, and the way he had shaped our thinking and our lives.

Chapter XXIII
I Finally Get Núñez's Published Book

Álvar Núñez Cabeza's narrative of his memorable journey across the North American continent was published in Spain in 1542, the year that the ailing Coronado had been carried on a litter through our Cáhita village of Zopa. He had called it *La Relación de Álvar Núñez Cabeza de Vaca.**

I was not able to find a copy until some time after I had begun to live in the City of Mexico. When finally I borrowed a copy, I read it with fascination many times. His days of trading and wandering inland and back to the coast were passed over lightly, except he told that he had suffered much in his days of servitude, during which he labored endlessly on menial tasks. One of his major occupations was digging, from cane swamps, the tubers the coastal Indians used as a mainstay of their diet. His hands and his feet remained raw and bleeding from this difficult work.

His days as a trader had become more bearable since he had been free to travel where he wished. Even so, his life had been

---

* Also called *Los Naufragios (The Shipwrecked Ones)*

one of exposure to storm and rain, which he mentioned but about which he did not complain. Núñez devoted only a few paragraphs to these several years of wandering.

He told simply of his work as a healer. He gave Castillo credit for being the first to go through healing rites in the village of the Avavares. But he added considerable detail describing his visit to the village of the Susolos and the incident where he prayed for the man who had been pronounced dead.

Nowhwere in his writing was there a hint of boastfulness. It is with deep humility that he recounted his great fame among the Indians and their near-worship of him. All was written in simple language, straightforward, factually just as I remembered it, but many times leaving out details that I remembered. Usually, he wrote vaguely about places so that it would be very difficult for anyone unfamiliar with the country to follow his route.

While laying no claims for his own greatness, a number of times he did express his gratitude to God for His grace and His blessing in helping him and guiding him in all that he did. Not once did he dramatize what had happened—one of the most dramatic series of events to take place in this part of the world. It was an overly modest account of highly significant achievements.

Knowing Núñez, the simplicity and matter-of-factness of his narrative was in character with the man. It had been his great faith in *el Bendito Dios* that had sustained him and made it possible for him to perform his great service of healing and teaching among the multitude of Indians he encountered in his long journeying.

As I read and reread this true story, once again the reality of its wonder and its unusual nature made itself clear to me. And as I read I realized with sadness and with a sense of great loss that I was never again to see this great man, a man of courage, of compassion, of triumphant faith and great vision.

Chapter XXIV
The Children of Darkness and the Child of the Sun

In my account of Núñez's last years I wish that I could write truthfully that he had gained in popularity and acceptance in his colony of Rio de la Plata. But, regretfully, I cannot do this.

For Ara and me, for Guatél and Maria, everything was satisfactory. My study of languages went well. I found that my knowledge of the language of the Chorrucas and of the Avavares gave me a foundation for the Coahuiltecan, since those two tribes spoke dialects of this language. And, of course, I knew the language of the Pueblos who lived on or near the Tiguex River.

After several intense years of study I became a teacher of Indian languages in the college in Mexico City. In spite of the many deficits in my knowledge and skills, I could cope with all this learning. My development in the life of learning, although gradual and slow, was the life that I had chosen to live. Of course, Núñez was responsible for the direction of my life. Without his teaching and influence I might have remained an itinerant trader for the rest of my life. And since I liked the life I had fallen into and felt the direction of my life was right, my gratitude and debt to him was great.

When I first arrived in Mexico City, Viceroy Mendoza had already laid plans for a college, later to become a university. As early as 1540 a temporary senior college of studies had been authorized. It was this college that both Guatél and I attended until we had finished.

When Luis de Velasco became viceroy, the university was authorized.* This was in 1557. In the same year Mendoza was sent to Lima. It was not until then that I took my advanced work for the highest degree. I was one of the first to receive the doctorate from the University of Mexico. This was the year Núñez died in Spain. Irala the unscrupulous, who had harmed Núñez so much, also died the same year.

True, my own life has become just what I wanted. Ara has been the right companion for me, and also gave me two fine sons who have been a constant joy to me. But what cannot end like a fairy tale is what happened to Núñez. I had vainly hoped he might return to Mexico. That was never to be.

Dorantes and Castillo never left Mexico. Each married a rich widow. Dorantes finally was father of eleven children, a whole village of his own! I heard little news of Castillo after his marriage, mostly from one man in Mexico City who informed me that Castillo's wife was no good, because the best she could do was to bear children that were all *mujeres* (women)! He told me that Castillo had a family of eleven girls! That, he said, was carrying a good thing too far!

After his return to Spain Núñez was evidently reunited with his wife, but I received no word of this. In fact, my knowledge of what happened to Núñez came from a variety of sources, including word-of-mouth reports, which we know may be most unreliable. About the final years of his life in Spain, however, I had a dependable, firsthand report.

Little by little, bit by bit, I have been able to piece together the last years of his career. And I shall tell them as I finally con-

---

* This summary of the beginning of the University of Mexico is taken from Juan Pablos, *The Dialogues of Cervantes de Salazar* (translated by Minnie Lee Barrett Shepherd), Austin, Texas: The University of Texas Press, 1953, p.6.

cluded that it all happened.

After I moved to the City of Mexico, I received news that Núñez had arrived in South America. All news was long in coming of course, offset by many delays. Finally, the official message came through that, in 1540, his appointment as *Adelantado*, Governor, Captain-General, and Chief Justice of Rio de la Plata had been confirmed. Such a title sounds pretentious, but its real meaning was that Núñez was to be the official head of government and leader of Rio de la Plata. There was a restricting condition, however. A man by the name of Juan de Ayolas had formerly held the position and was presumably killed. Núñez had been appointed with the stipulation that if de Ayolas was still alive, he would continue as governor-general. When it became certain that de Ayolas was dead, confirmation of Núñez as governor was finalized. De Ayolas had been the typical avaricious, self-seeking Spanish conquistador, and seemingly a majority of the colonists in Rio de la Plata were of the same character. The corrupt nature of the colonists of Rio de la Plata was what really defeated Núñez. Núñez, an altogether different breed, was obviously one whom the colonists would not understand and would not like.

It is clear that Núñez was headed for the worst kind of trouble. Knowing Núñez and his idealism, I feel that he was confident that his attitude of goodwill toward all men would conquer in the long run. Perhaps he was right. Sometimes the long run is very long; in his case, it was longer than the remainder of his earthly life.

When he left Mexico, Núñez was in middle-life and was physically strong and vital. But several years had gone by before his appointment as Governor-General of Rio de la Plata—many delays before sailing; a trip to South America and finally to Asunción, the seat of government of the colony, which took a long time. Núñez, however, was apparently still rugged and tough physically. His boat landed at Santa Catalina Island on the east coast of South America. As I look at the map the distance from the island to Asunción is roughly 600 leagues in a direct line. Núñez followed a much longer way, his route curving far to the north before it turned south again and then went almost directly to Asunción.

It was told that Núñez made most of this first journey barefooted. He said he did this to set an inspiring example for his men. It had the opposite effect, causing his men to ridicule him. I have wondered if this was not his attempt to reenact his triumphal journey through the Indian villages of Mexico, which was the highest point in his life. Regardless of his intent, Núñez had misjudged the men he was leading. They held him up to scorn for such an un-European action.

On this trip his treatment of the Indians, the Guaranís, was uniformly kind. The natives responded to this as they had in Mexico, with friendship and generosity. Later, when the worst happened to Núñez, the Guaranís could not understand the harsh treatment of such a good man by his fellow countrymen.

Núñez landed on Santa Catalina Island in 1541. With him came two monks, named Armenta and Lebrón, whom he had found on the mainland. These two men held the natives in contempt. They consorted sexually with native women. Apparently, they sought only the gratification of their own desires. Such men would be expected to sneer at one with the strict standards and high ideals of Núñez. And so it turned out, because they became his open enemies, and undermined him at every opportunity.

Núñez's real trouble on his first journey came from his own men. The natives were good-natured and helpful. They brought food to Núñez and guided him through the jungle. They were amazed and terrified by the horses of the Spaniards. This was the usual reaction of people who had not seen horses before. But the soldiers had expected to gratify themselves with Indian women and with loot. Núñez forbade both of these, and enforced his discipline. The two monks rebelled against his rigorous standards, and escaped ahead with other malcontents. They pillaged the villages and otherwise followed the vagaries of their own lusts.

Núñez promptly indicted them, but they successfully disappeared into the forests. Since he could not find them, nothing ever came of the indictment. Later, these two unscrupulous monks reappeared and Núñez allowed them to accompany him on an expedition to the interior.

Núñez built many bridges, crossed high mountains, waded through dismal swamps, and hacked his way through endless miles of tangled jungle. The route was beset by a multitude of physical difficulties. And Núñez triumphed over them all, with the exception of the enmity of his own soldiers.

Victoriously, Núñez reached Asunción after a journey considered impossible. He felt God was blessing him as he sought to lead his people in honesty, fairness and goodness. There is no denying his initial triumph. Even in Mexico, people spoke in terms of amazement at such a journey. But this was not sufficient, for already there were combined evil forces at work that rebelled against Núñez's goodness and high ideals.

The acting-governor upon Núñez's arrival was Irala, a man who had been in the favor of de Ayolas. Irala's behavior was almost beyond imagination. He kept a harem of Indian girls as concubines and sold them for his own enrichment. There had been murders and rapes which Irala either condoned or openly approved. In a futile attempt to placate Irala's followers, Núñez appointed Irala his first-lieutenant and adjutant. This was probably a grievous error, since it was interpreted as weakness. Open opposition might have been wiser.

Núñez's attempts at justice in the colony and his rule against slavery, coupled with other high standards, only angered the colonists. Practically all of them had come to South America for the most selfish reasons. They felt Núñez was a self-righteous prig, and they were willing to go to any extreme to defeat him. They accused him of aspiring to be King of Rio de la Plata and of becoming a tyrant.

Núñez undertook a hazardous trip to the interior. Part of it was by boat, but he later went many days on foot. During this expedition they lived chiefly on tropical fruit. He would have penetrated farther west and possibly even reached Peru, had not his fellow explorers, who were as usual interested in loot and lust, voted to return. When they returned to their boat, they found food scarce and hostile Indians threatening them. Most of the friendly Indians who had accompanied them had by now deserted them.

Nearly all the men were stricken with fever, probably malaria.

Núñez was sick for weeks and what he did at that time was probably a result of his delirium and extreme weakness. At last, in
a more lucid brief period, he ordered the boat back to Asunción.

During this expedition, Núñez had come under increasing
disfavor. Life for these men had become a prolonged punishment, and his men blamed him for all their physical difficulties.
Back in Asunción, Núñez, still feverridden, was confined to his
bed.

Irala and a number of fellow conspirators mobbed Núñez
while he was still bedridden and too weak to stand. Although
they threatened his life and imprisoned him, they were afraid
to murder him in cold blood. Irala was proclaimed governor by
the unprincipled colonists.

When the Indians heard that Núñez was imprisoned and was
accused of being a wicked man, they openly protested. While
this was a great compliment, and showed Núñez's real
character, it could do no good; the Indians had neither power nor
influence with the Spaniards.

Paraguay became an extremely lawless land again. The lust
of the Spaniards knew no bounds. Irala established his harem
only two leagues from Asunción. The two dissolute monks,
Armenta and Lebrón, joined forces with the rebels; they condemned Núñez and sang their own hymns of self-praise to the
king. Then they set off for Catalina Island with half a hundred
young Indian girls manacled together for the entire march.
There seemed no doubt about their evil use of these girls.

About this time in Mexico, Fray José had been called back to
Spain—to Madrid. He told me, "I don't know much about why
I am being sent back. My heart is here in Mexico and I shall
plan to return." As it happened, it was providential that he did
travel to Madrid.

It was in 1543 when Núñez was mobbed, cruelly mistreated
and kept as a prisoner in his house, guarded day and night. For
almost two years he was kept prisoner and in April of 1545 he
was sent back to Spain, accused of treason. The unprincipled
Irala had won out largely because he was supported by nearly
all the colonists.

Between the sad, sordid lines of Núñez's betrayal and defeat,

I read another story: He went to Paraguay with the dream of a paradise on earth created by God's love. He dreamed of a colony of Spaniards, good, upright people, fair-minded, and just, living adjacent to Indians in peace and harmony. He had visions of the humanitarian treatment of the Indians, and opportunities for them to make the most of their lives. It was really a dream of the Kingdom of God on earth, which is the kingdom of goodness. Núñez worked hard for the materialization of his dream, but the dream was shattered by evil, self-seeking men.

I grieved for this great, good man, the best man I had ever known. Perhaps he was the best man on earth in his day.

*   *   *

For myself and Ara and our two boys, all is well. Gradually, over the years, I grew increasingly grateful for a good mind and the ability to learn, to think straight, and to teach. My size ceased long ago to be a problem to me.

Thinking of the world realistically, I know how impossible was Núñez's dream. Yet I am glad to have witnessed the Great Spirit working through such a man. Evil men defeated Núñez in Rio de la Plata.

With this thought in mind, I am suddenly reminded of a legend I had heard in the village of the Avavares long ago: The Avavares told about a being whom they said was a man, and whom they called Bad Thing. This strange being would appear mysteriously in the doorway of a lodge in their village. The people of that lodge were evidently paralyzed with fear, since they could not resist Bad Thing. They would submit to anything he wanted to do to them.

They said that he would usually pick out a victim. Using a large flint knife, he would cut open the victim's abdomen and cut off a section of his intestines. He would throw that into the fire. Then with the same large, crude knife he would make deep incisions in the victim's arms. Sometimes he would entirely sever an arm from the rest of the body.

Then he would lay his hands on all the wounds, or replace the severed arm, and the victim's body would heal almost instantly.

The Indians marveled at the rapidity of the healing.

Several times they said that they had offered him food, but he would never eat. When they asked him where he came from, he would point to a crack in the earth and say that he lived below and came from below.

Another act of Bad Thing was to cause a lodge to be lifted high in the air and then let it fall, smashing down to earth again.

Núñez and his companions, myself included, had greeted this story with loud laughter. This skepticism caused the Avavares to bring to the Spaniards a number of people with scars on their abdomens and arms, which they vowed were the scars from the wounds Bad Thing inflicted.

Our ridicule gave way. Before us were a number of people with clear scars of healing. Did I believe their bizarre story? Do I today? I just don't know.

One thing I do know is that there is evil in the world in which we live. I wish to have nothing to do with it, nor with the people who live by it and serve it, as did Irala and his co-conspirators in Paraguay. Whatever I may or may not believe about Bad Thing, I know that the harm that came from Irala and his associates is much worse than what Bad Thing reportedly did.

Irala and most of the European inhabitants of Rio de la Plata physically mistreated Núñez. They lied about him to the Council of the Indies. And according to many reports they put poison in his food so that for a long time he lingered just short of death. All this because they rejected Núñez's goodness, his insistence on justice and fairness toward all people. The harm they did him is immeasurable in its consequences: their false accusations against him changed not only the attitude of the Council of the Indies toward him, but also that of the people of Spain, and to some extent the historians who have written about Núñez.

Núñez was sent back to Spain for trial. False witnesses were procured by torment and by force. The signatures of one hundred thirty-two colonists were obtained without their knowing what statements they were signing. Most of these accusations were fabricated after the prison ship was crossing the ocean.

Before the Council of the Indies was laid a great bundle of condemning testimonies. Núñez was indicted and tried. Thirty-four

serious charges were filed against him. He was thrown into jail
in Madrid. Later, though, he was detained in an inn of Madrid
and not permitted to leave it. He was pronounced guilty.

Núñez, however, filed countersuits, and the trial continued
year after year. Final judgment and condemnation did not come
until 1551. Núñez appealed his case.

When Fray José returned to Mexico City, he gave me the story
of Núñez's final days. "It was after long imprisonment, when
Núñez was around 60 years of age, that he was released from
jail. I had visited him often. He was destitute and ill. In the eyes
of most of Spain he was a failure and legally condemned.

"But you can rest assured that this good man was always true
to his ideals. He told me, 'None of my trials or suffering can compare with those of Jesu-Cristo. If he could stand them, I can
stand what is being done to me.' His faith in God carried him
through everything. I befriended him and enjoyed many long
visits with him.

"His greatest joy came from his memory of his long journey
among the Indians of Mexico as he became the first Spaniard to
cross the continent. He frequently talked of you, whom he
always called Cazador. He was happy about your success in the
university as a teacher.

"He wanted to clear his name of the charges against him, and
so did his wife. He appealed his case. But this was hopeless. No
one from Rio de la Plata rallied to his defense. There were thirty
charges against him fictitiously signed by the colonists. The
Council of the Indies was impressed by the sheer volume of the
sheaf of written charges.

"I am glad that I could be with Núñez just before he died. I ad-
ministered the last rites and could tell he was grateful, as was
his wife. I believe I was sent to Spain to minister to and comfort
this great man of God."

When I heard of Núñez's death even before Fray José came
back to Mexico, I felt stricken with sadness for many days. I
could understand the Indians' near-worship of this man since
I, too, felt this way. So I wrote a short verse expressing how I felt
in Spanish, which had become the language I spoke most of
the time.

Núñez, Núñez, mi maestro,
Mi corazon se me quebra
Por tí,
Mis lagrimas caen
Como la lluvia
Por tí.

(Núñez, Núñez, my teacher
My heart breaks for you
My tears fall
Like the rain
For you.)

Later, our university received a book from Spain that corroborated the conclusions I had come to about Núñez's mistreatment and shameful betrayal in Rio de la Plata. It was *Los Commentarios de Núñez Cabeza de Vaca,* written by Pero Hernandez, and published in Valladolid in 1555. It did not reach us at the University of Mexico until a year after publication. And, though it added little to what I already knew, a series of events mentioned by Hernandez attracted my attention. Núñez had gone on his voyage of discovery to the heart of the continent, as I knew. When he left the port of Los Reyes to go back to Asunción, he ordered his men to return all their concubines to their families. There were about 100 of these girls. This angered the Spaniards, who wanted them. Still, Núñez enforced his orders and the girls were returned to their families. Hernandez attributed a great deal of the colonists' later vindictiveness toward Núñez to this. For me this important detail fit perfectly into the pattern of high standards Núñez tried to uphold, and which had aroused so much hostility against him.

It seems to me as I read and study, that an interesting series of repetitions has occurred in the history of mankind. As much as I have read, I know that I am still unaware of a great deal that has happened; perhaps information is yet unavailable to me. But from what I know, periodically there have appeared great teachers and great servants of mankind. I have read the life of **Gautama** Buddha who lived centuries before Christ. Sketchily,

I have read of one even before **Gautama**, named Krishna. I am sure there have been many others.

Through Núñez and Fray José and from my own reading in *El Nuevo Testamento*, I have learned a great deal about Jesu-Cristo. He was called the Son of God and the Light of the World. It was he who inspired Núñez to do his work of healing and teaching among the Indians north of the Rio Grande and in western Mexico. He chose to die on the cross rather than use force to conquer his enemies. His followers wrote that he was resurrected from the grave—that the life of God in him was so powerful that death and the grave were conquered. Jesu-Cristo was the greatest of all the great teachers.

Here in Mexico the Nahuas have an old oral tradition about a great teacher whom they call Quetzalcoatl. He lived first among the Mayas, who called him Kulkulcan. According to tradition he taught the people of Mexico many things about the stars and planets and mathematics. He is said to have been the first to introduce *mais* (corn) to Mexico, and also the use of rubber. He taught the arts and sciences and the worship of the one true God, who he called *Ometeotl*. That must have been thousands of years ago, since *mais* has been the chief food of Mexico for several thousand years.

What strikes me personally is that Quetzalcoatl was said to have had many dwarfs and hunchbacks in his court. Perhaps through him the Indians of Mexico honor me, a dwarf!

Quetzalcoatl told the people of Mexico, as he left from the east, that he would come again. Jesu-Cristo told his disciples before his ascension that he would come again.

My own idea is that from time to time through history, the Great Spirit shows His concern and his love for mankind by sending these great teachers, healers, and leaders. The promise is always "I will come again." I think the Great Spirit comes again and again and again.

I also think He comes to any who wish to receive Him. Thus we have had many Cristos, anointed ones, and shall have others. And there is a Cristo in each of us when we recognize the Great Spirit. I think back on Akka's wonderful treatment of me, her motherly love for me, and complete acceptance of me. This, too, was a manifestation of the Great Spirit. This is the Cristo in human beings, everyday common people!

My own awareness of the Great Spirit is the most important aspect of my life. It came to me gradually. I was only faintly acquainted with this idea before I met Núñez, but through him this awareness grew. As I saw him healing people and teaching people, my knowledge grew even more. In Akka I also experienced the Spirit's presence, this time in the life of a humble, but wonderful woman.

Then, when I went back to my people and taught them and felt their love and respect, my spiritual insight became intense. As I traveled through the *Jornado del Muerto* and across the desert to overtake Núñez, my sense of a real Presence was constant and radiant and beautiful in my life and in everything about me. Núñez was touched and possessed by deity. His leader and teacher was Jesu-Cristo. Núñez recognized his kinship with Jesu-Cristo. Núñez lived the life of Cristo among us.

Perhaps my grief and my desolation that Núñez died destitute, lonely, brokenhearted, and unrecognized is all wrong. These circumstances are only transitory, just as the crucifixion and death of Jesu-Cristo was only transitory. The important concerns of Núñez's life—his relation with the Great Spirit and his dedication to the loving service of mankind—these are what endure.

About the Author

Frank Cheavens, born in June 1905, has been teaching in the psychology department at The University of Texas at Arlington for the past 27 years. After completing his undergraduate studies at Baylor University, he went on to obtain his M.A. and Ph.D. at The University of Texas at Austin. Now retired with the rank of professor emeritus, he teaches part time in the field of psychotherapy and psychotherapeutic counseling and is a grandfather of four.

Dr. Cheavens' diverse interests include astronomy, religion wildlife (especially wolves), birds, fish, nutrition, exercise, and history. He has written and lectured extensively on the history of Texas and the Southwest. His published poetry, short stories, serials, and articles have appeared in numerous magazines and scholarly journals, including *New Century Leader, Field and Stream, Nature,* and *Christian Science Monitor.* He has served as outdoor editor of *Texas Parade,* author of two brochures on mental health, and editor of the *Harlingen Report,* which documents action research in educational and civic contexts in South Texas.

A prolific writer, Frank Cheavens is also the author of *Arrow Lie Still* (1950), *Vernacular Languages and Education* (1957), and *How to Stop Feeling Blue* (1971), which has been reprinted in a number of languages.